"Look—" Alexa held her hands up as if to placate him "—I'm not talking about a real marriage. I'm talking about a temporary engagement that works for us both."

"As far as proposals go, this one is definitely novel, but marriage—sorry, engagement—doesn't work for me at all. Temporary or not."

"I know." She gave a heavy sigh, tucking a strand of thick, silky hair that had come loose back behind her ear. She looked gloriously mussed from where his hands had been and that reminded Rafa of how much he'd like to put them there again. Unwind all that magnificent hair and find out how long it was.

As if they had a will of their own, his eyes followed her as she paced the mahogany-decked reading room, her gown hugging her heavenly curves as she moved. "That's why I chose you."

With two university degrees and a variety of false career starts under her belt, **Michelle Conder** decided to satisfy her lifelong desire to write and finally found her dream job. She currently lives in Melbourne, Australia, with one super-indulgent husband, three self-indulgent (but exquisite) children, a menagerie of overindulged pets and the intention of doing some form of exercise daily. She loves to hear from her readers at michelleconder.com.

Books by Michelle Conder

Harlequin Presents

Duty at What Cost?
The Most Expensive Lie of All
Hidden in the Sheikh's Harem
Defying the Billionaire's Command
The Italian's Virgin Acquisition
The Billionaire's Virgin Temptation

Conveniently Wed!

Bound to Her Desert Captor

One Night With Consequences

Prince Nadir's Secret Heir

The Chatsfield

Russian's Ruthless Demand

Visit the Author Profile page
at Harlequin.com for more titles.

Michelle Conder

THEIR ROYAL WEDDING BARGAIN

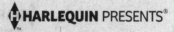

HARLEQUIN PRESENTS®

Recycling programs
for this product may
not exist in your area.

ISBN-13: 978-1-335-89338-3

Their Royal Wedding Bargain

First North American publication 2019

Copyright © 2019 by Michelle Conder

Printed in U.S.A.

THEIR ROYAL WEDDING
BARGAIN

To Heather—for years of love and friendship, and for always being in my corner. I'll always be in yours, too.

And to my dad. There just wasn't enough time in the end. I miss you.

CHAPTER ONE

TONIGHT WAS GOING to be a total disaster. Alexa could *feel* it.

The Annual Santarian Children's Charity ball, one of the most prestigious events on the international calendar, would commence in under an hour, and she felt sick with apprehension.

'He's here, Your Highness,' Nasrin, her assistant-cum-lady's-maid-cum-devoted-companion, murmured as she closed the bedroom door, a ripple of excitement evident in her quick steps as she returned to Alexa. 'One of the chambermaids confirmed that the Prince of Santara has just entered the Summer Palace.'

Retrieving the hairbrush from the old-fashioned vanity unit, Nasrin picked up a skein of Alexa's long dark hair and met her wide-eyed gaze in the mirror. 'This is so exciting. I can't believe you're actually going to do it.'

Alexa couldn't either; releasing a measured breath at the thought of what she intended to do, followed swiftly by the seizing of her stomach.

Known for her cool, unflappable poise under pressure, she felt as if she was about to throw up the grilled cheese sandwich she'd had for lunch all over her custom-made designer gown.

He was here. He was really here.

Prince Rafaele of Santara, the King's younger brother, had actually arrived. There had been whispers that he might not attend tonight, given that he'd created a scandal at this very event last year, embarrassing the King. But apparently nothing stopped the Rebel Prince of Santara from following his own path, and that was a trait that could work in her favour tonight so she should see it as a positive. Being a determined rule follower, she found that somewhat difficult, adding to her massive sense of self-doubt.

How was she going to do it? How was she going to ask a prince with the reputation as a consummate playboy to marry her, even if she was a princess herself? Because that was what she intended to do. What she *had* to do if she wanted to appease her father.

She and Nasrin had hatched the crazy eleventh-hour plan to propose a fake marriage—or engagement because, as she would explain to the Prince, she had no intention of actually going through with the wedding—two weeks ago when she had realised that her father was deadly serious about seeing her married as soon as possible.

Of course she'd tried to argue with him. Tell him that she wasn't ready, that she needed more time, but he had shaken his head and informed her that nothing she said would change his mind. As the Crown Princess of Berenia, and only remaining heir, he would not rest until she was settled.

To be fair he had given her six months to create a list of possible marriageable contenders, but Alexa had dragged her feet, hoping he would forget all about it. On the night he'd told her he hadn't forgotten at all, she and Nasrin had sat down to commiserate over a glass of Sauterne and a completely unrealistic rom-com at the end of a long working day.

According to Nasrin the main actor looked like the dreamy Santarian Prince, his character replete with arrogant, bad boy tendencies and a super-hot body, and the idea had been born. In the film the hero had not wanted to marry the heroine, but love had won out in the end.

Alexa knew from past experience that love rarely won out in the end, but fortunately that wasn't what she required from the Prince.

'It's going to be fine, Princess Alexa; he'll do it,' Nasrin murmured, accurately reading the panic in her eyes for what it was. 'Then you'll have everything your heart desires.'

Everything her heart desired?

What she desired the most was time to make her own marriage match, and for her older brother to still be alive.

Sol had been the true heir to the Berenian throne but since his tragic death three years ago that duty had fallen to her. And she wasn't up to it, not yet anyway, and deep down she wondered if her father believed that she wasn't up to it either, especially after the serious lapse in judgement she'd made when she was seventeen. Perhaps that was one of the reasons he was pushing so hard for her to marry right now. Why he was so determined to have it done.

That, and to remove the stink of shame that still hovered over her after the King of Santara had abruptly ended their betrothal twelve months earlier. The ink hadn't even dried on their marriage contract before he had pulled out and immediately married another woman—an outsider, no less—his actions stirring up centuries-old animosity between their nations and giving the BLF—the Berenian Liberation Front—just the excuse they needed to re-engage in hostilities with Santara.

Her and King Jaeger's brief, ill-fated betrothal hadn't been a love-match by any stretch, but his rejection had still felt like yet another kick in the teeth for Alexa because she had *liked* him. She'd developed a massive crush on King Jaeger when he had saved her from an embarrassing experience on her first official engagement as her father's consort. At thirteen, she'd been so nervous, decked out in a white tulle gown that had made her feel like a beautiful fairy, that she'd accidentally upended a full jug of cranberry juice all over herself. She'd frozen to the spot as the cold, sticky red liquid had drenched the front of her beautiful gown and chilled her skin. Before she'd been able to respond the newly crowned King of Santara had stepped in behind her and enveloped her in his jacket and whispered that everything would be okay.

Mortified, Alexa had buried her scalding cheeks against his chest, allowing him to draw her from the room without anyone really noticing them. He'd instructed a servant to find her lady's maid and then melted back into the party. Alexa hadn't drunk cranberry juice since, and nor had she forgotten the King's kindness. As she'd matured he'd become the epitome of her dream man: kind, loyal, compassionate and strong.

His brother, by contrast, couldn't be more different. The consummate good-time guy, Prince Rafaele moved from one lissom blonde to the next as if he was doing nothing more important than choosing a new tie to wear with his suit.

'Having your hair up was a good choice,' Nasrin said as she twisted the last of Alexa's waist-length tresses into place. 'It shows off the sheer panelling at the back of your dress to perfection.'

'It's not too revealing, is it?' Alexa murmured, twisting on her padded stool to get a better view. She'd chosen her nude-coloured off-the-shoulder gown to attract as much attention as she dared, but she wasn't used to wearing clothing that revealed so much skin.

'Not at all. It's perfect.'

Alexa stared at her carefully made-up face with critical indifference. Perfect would be to have the task ahead of her put behind her and sorted to her satisfaction.

'And you're sure he doesn't want to get married?' she asked, her outward calm slipping ever so slightly. One of the things that made the Prince so perfect was his reported disinclination to marry. If he didn't want to marry he would never want to make their union permanent and interfere with her chance to do things her way.

'Absolutely.' Nasrin nodded. 'He's been on record as saying he never intends to marry. Not that the women seem to be listening. They throw themselves at him like lemmings off a cliff, hoping to be the one to change his mind.'

So why did she feel so sick?

Probably because actually attracting the attention of a man like the Prince was completely foreign to her, thanks to her father's strict rules and regulations, and her own sense of inadequacy with men. Not that she'd always felt that way. Once, when she was seventeen, she'd believed a man—Stefano—had found her beautiful. But what he'd really found was that she was gullible. Gullible enough to be seduced by a man who was more interested in her title than her as a woman. The mistake had hit her budding confidence hard, pushing her to focus on her degree in business management, and her royal duties, to the exclusion of all else.

Not that she wanted to *attract* Prince Rafaele. No, she only wanted his cooperation in a scheme that, in the end, would serve him as equally as it would her by restoring cordial relations between their two nations. A scheme that had seemed a lot easier to follow through on when she'd gone over it late at night in her bed than in the cold light of day.

Trying to remain positive, Alexa slipped on her heels and smoothed her hands down her bespoke gown, ignoring how the clever creation made her feel both elegant *and* naked—which, according to her exuberant assistant, was the whole point of the design.

'You will feel sexy and alluring,' Nasrin had assured her when she'd first set eyes on the dress. 'And every man in the room will look at you and want you.'

Right now she felt as sexy and alluring as a tree. And she didn't want *every* man in the room looking at her. She was nervous enough thinking about *one* man looking at her.

She picked up the dossier Nasrin had put together on Prince Rafaele last week, rifling through photo after photo of him attending parties and movie premieres every other week. Vastly wealthy in his own right, he owned an empire of nightclubs and bars across Europe that, once opened, became the only place to be seen. *'Dens of iniquity*, her father had once disparaged.

An unwanted shiver shot through her as she gazed at a shirtless photo of the Prince holding onto a sail line on the deck of a yacht. His white trousers were flattened against his muscular thighs by the breeze, his dark shoulder-length hair streaming out behind him, his broad chest deeply tanned to the colour of the teak deck. His face was turned towards the camera and the lens had lovingly captured his perfect wide smile, hawkish features and startling blue eyes as he laughed at something in the distance.

The caption underneath read: *The Rebel Prince in search of sun, fun and adventure.*

Alexa studied his image. Despite his relaxed pose there was something about the way he held himself that said *Danger…beware.* A jaded slant to his lips that indicated that he had seen everything there was to see in life, and was surprised by none of it. Which would be a good thing if he went along with her plan because their break-up would seem inevitable: the Playboy Prince and the shrinking violet could never have lasted. Not that she *was* a shrinking violet. She just chose not to make waves if she didn't have to.

'Hot, isn't he?' Nasrin said as she glanced at the photo before running a practised eye over Alexa. 'You look stunning, Your Highness. The Prince won't be able to resist you.'

While Alexa appreciated Nasrin's optimism, she knew from personal experience that men found her all too easy to resist. 'More likely he'll laugh in my face.' She closed the file. 'And if he's that opposed to marriage he might not even go for a temporary engagement.'

'But you have an ace up your sleeve. If he agrees, it could help settle all the bad blood between our nations. Of course he'll go for that. And the engagement would only be temporary. Unless...' Nasrin's pretty eyes sparkled mischievously '...you fall in love with each other.'

Alexa shook her head. Nasrin had a romantic nature that no amount of rational conversation could extinguish. And while Alexa might have once craved love and a happy-ever-after too, she'd been disappointed enough in the past not to wait around for it.

Love wasn't as important as dignity. Self-respect. Objectivity. And imagining the Prince of Santara falling in love with her, or her with him, was frankly hilarious.

'That's as likely to happen as the moon is to turn blue,' she said dryly.

'If you wish hard enough, Your Highness, you'll get whatever you ask for.'

Alexa knew that rarely happened either.

'Fortunately, I don't want the Prince's love. Just his co-operation.'

'Then go get it,' Nasrin urged with a flourish.

Alexa smiled. Nasrin had been like a gift when she'd come to work for her after Sol had died, organising her life and making her smile again with her chatty, easy nature. Everything else had felt so oppressive at the time, oppressive and overwhelming, during those dark days.

Not that she begrudged her role as the future Queen of Berenia. She didn't because she loved her country, and her countrymen, and she wanted to do the best job for them in Sol's stead. She wanted to make her father proud. And if the Prince went along with her plan she could do that. She could help rebuild relations between Berenia and Santara, and buy herself the necessary time to make a marriage that not only pleased her father but herself as well.

The decider would be whether or not she could

implement a plan that had seemed perfectly logical at inception, but now felt desperately naive.

But if the Prince turned her down she'd just have to find someone else. Because the alternative—marrying the man who was on top of her father's list of eligible suitors—didn't bear thinking about.

Rafe gazed around the ballroom of the Santarian Summer Palace, a place he'd spent many formative years, with mixed emotions. As a general rule he tried not to return here very often, not only because it didn't hold the best memories, but because when he'd left Santara as a disaffected teenager he'd cut all ties with his nation.

And he wasn't sorry that he had. He didn't miss the life here. He didn't miss the sun that was hot enough most of the year to blister paint, and he didn't miss the endless round of lacklustre royal duties his father had expected him to carry out as the second son of Santara. The less important son. He didn't miss having his ideas shot down in flames by a man who had never understood his drive and ambition to forge his own path in life.

'It's lucky you're a prince, sibi,' his father had often snarled. *'You'd amount to nothing if you weren't.'*

Hard-nosed and narrow-minded, his father had

treated opposing opinions as little more than ripples on a quiet pond.

Rafe had learned not to care, disconnecting from his father, and rubbing his nose in it any chance that he got. And despite—or perhaps because of—his father's convictions that he wouldn't amount to anything he'd made a success of his life.

He'd broken free of the constraints of royal duty and lived life on his own terms. Not that his father was around to see it. His death when Rafe had been eighteen was the very thing that had set him free. Or rather his brother had set him free when he'd stepped into the role of King at nineteen and given Rafe permission to spread his wings.

Returning from studying in the US at the time, Rafe knew that Jag could have used his insider knowledge and support, and it was only now, looking back, that he understood the sacrifice his brother had made for him, shouldering the burden of a troubled nation on his own and never asking anything of Rafe in return.

Once sharing what he would have said was an unbreakable bond, their relationship had grown strained with distance and Rafe was never sure how to bridge the gulf without losing himself in the process. Still, he owed Jag a debt of gratitude, even if his brother didn't think so.

Catching the direction of his thoughts before they progressed any further, Rafe shook them off with well-practised ease. This was partly the reason he hated returning home. The memories, the choked feeling of constraint and the heaviness that came over him that wasn't a part of the life that he lived now. A life based on unsurpassed pleasure, beauty and freedom. A life he lived predominantly in England, where he'd used a stellar investment in technology while attending Cambridge to purchase his first bar and nightclub. He had 'the touch' some said, an innate ability to tap into what his clientele wanted and to transform any venue he took over into the hottest place in town.

Which often made *him* the hottest *property* in town, pursued again and again by women looking to change his mind about remaining single. Something he had no intention of doing. Ever. In his experience the novelty factor rarely lasted beyond the bedroom and, even if it did, his parents' tumultuous relationship had cured him of ever thinking marriage was an institution he wanted to be part of.

Much better to have fun while it lasted, and move on before anyone got hurt. And if the tabloids wanted to paint him as a playboy prince to get foot traffic on their websites, that was hardly his problem. Something Jag didn't understand.

But then Jag was still a little aggrieved about the whole French heiress debacle at this event last year. Having grown bored early on in the night, Rafe had taken her to his hot tub upstairs, only to have her post photos of the two of them to her social media account. If he'd known Jag was in the middle of important negotiations with her father at the time he would have insisted that she leave her phone downstairs.

An oversight that had led him to promise his brother that he would stay out of trouble this evening. Which wasn't exactly fair because Rafe rarely went looking for trouble any more. More often than not it found him.

As if on cue, he saw his sister making a beeline for him as she wound her way through the throng of impeccably groomed guests at the ball.

'I take it the ostrich lost?' he teased, his eyes going to the brightly coloured feathers covering her skirt. 'Or do you have plans to return the outfit to the poor creature at the end of the night?'

'Laugh all you want,' Milena challenged with narrowed eyes. 'But I love the dress and every feather had already been shed before it was collected. Is that what you were grinning at before? Or was it something else? I swear you had that glint in your eye that said you were up to no good.'

'Just remembering a certain French heiress I met at about this time last year.'

'Oh, please.' Milena rolled her eyes. 'Don't let Jag hear you say the words "French" and "heiress" together in a sentence; he'll blow a gasket.'

'He needs to loosen up. He got the deal with her father through in the end so it was a win-win for both of us.'

'No thanks to you,' she retorted. 'When are you going to start dating women you respect *and* want to—'

'Don't say it.' Rafe shuddered. 'I like to imagine that you're still innocent of such matters. And anyway, I promised our esteemed brother that I'd be on my best behaviour tonight, so don't worry.'

He gave his sister his trademark grin, knowing that it wouldn't work one bit. She might be six years younger than his thirty years but she'd always had his measure.

'That only makes me worry more.' She groaned. 'And, speaking of Jag, you need to cut him some slack. He's got a lot on his plate right now.'

'Like?'

'The Berenian thing.'

'Still?' Rafe arched a brow. He knew Berenia was causing problems but he'd thought that would have died down by now. 'So he didn't marry their revered Princess last year. They need to move on and get over it.'

'There's more to it than that. Santara has advanced much further on the world stage than Berenia, which brings its own set of resentments.'

'Yes, but still their incompetence can hardly be our problem.'

'I don't know the ins and outs of it but… Oh, there's Jag, looking for us. I was supposed to find you so we can get the official photos out of the way.'

'Lead on,' Rafe said with amusement. He'd smile and play nice so his brother would have nothing to grumble about at the end of the night. Then tomorrow he'd fly home and resume his normal life, which wasn't dictated by pomp or protocol.

'Rafa.' Jag greeted him with a hint of stiffness. 'I wasn't sure you were going to make it this year.'

'Never miss it. Especially if there's a French heiress to be had.'

'Rafa!' Milena scolded under her breath. 'You promised.'

Rafe laughed. 'Don't worry. Jag knows I'm joking.'

'Jag hopes you're joking,' his brother muttered. 'And just because you made a career out of annoying our father don't feel that you have to carry the tradition on with me because I'm King.'

'Wouldn't dream of it.' Rafe grinned. 'I hear you're having some issues with the Berenians.'

'Don't mention that word. I swear they're the most stubborn people on earth.'

A photographer stopped in front of them. 'The lighting is probably better over by the far column, Your Majesty; do you mind moving in that direction?'

'Not at all,' Jag said, casting his eyes across the sea of chattering guests until he spotted what he was looking for. He crooked his finger, a small smile playing at the edges of his mouth, softening his face in a way Rafe had rarely seen before. Following his line of sight, he watched as Jag's new wife made her way towards them. Clearly pregnant, in a slim-fitting gown, she looked beautiful and only had eyes for his brother.

When she reached his side, Rafe could have sworn the rest of the room dissolved for both of them. Bemused, he wondered what it felt like to want someone that much, and then decided he didn't want to know.

'Good evening, Your Majesty,' Rafe greeted his new Queen. 'You're looking as beautiful as ever.' He took her hand and raised it to his lips. 'Should you ever tire of my stiff-necked brother, you only have to—'

'Rafa—' Jag began warningly.

Queen Regan laughed softy and placed her hand on his brother's arm. 'Always the devil, Rafaele.' She smiled at him. 'It's a skill to make a pregnant woman blush. But where is your date tonight? I understand you're seeing a Spanish supermodel. Ella? Or Esme?'

'Estela,' Rafe corrected.

'My apologies.' She glanced around curiously. 'Did you bring her with you?'

'Unfortunately, we had a difference in priorities and parted ways.'

'And you're clearly crestfallen.' Regan arched a brow, a playful glow in her eyes. 'Do I want to know what those priorities were?'

'If you two are quite finished flirting,' Jag said with an edge of menace in his voice, 'the photographer is waiting.'

'Sorry.' Regan threaded her arm through his. 'But I'm a married woman now. I have to live vicariously and Rafaele always has such *interesting* stories.'

'I'll give you an interesting story later on,' Jag promised throatily. 'For now just smile and imagine it.'

'Whatever they have, I don't want it,' Rafe grouched, lining up on the other side of his sister.

'It's called love,' Milena said impishly. 'And I can't wait to experience it.'

'Just don't fall in love with anyone I haven't checked out first,' Rafe warned sternly.

'Oh, fiddle.' She waved him away. 'You and Jag are as bad as each other. You're more alike than you might think.'

She was wrong. It had always been easier to be the bad to Jag's good. But he didn't offer an objection. Instead he pasted a smile on his face and pinched his sister's side just as the photographer clicked the shutter. Milena kicked his ankle in return and it was their usual game on to see who could make the other break first.

Two hours later, bored to the bone, Rafe thought about heading to his hot tub—alone—when he saw her. A vision who appeared to be nude at first glance but who, unfortunately, wasn't. But she was breathtaking, with her dark hair, smooth caramel skin and elegant cameo-like profile. Her delicate features were complemented by slender curves and long legs.

They'd fit, he realised with a jolt, somehow already knowing just how good they would be together though he'd never even spoken to her. Instantly intrigued by the notion that he wanted to know the colour of her eyes and the taste of her lips under his. He wanted to feel her warm silken skin and feast his eyes on her sweet curves as he stripped that clever gown from her body with aching slowness for the very first time.

As if sensing the heat of his thoughts, she turned her head, her eyes instantly finding his.

She blinked, as if she felt the caress of the erotic images coursing through his brain, a flush touching her high cheekbones. Or was that just his imagination going overboard? It certainly couldn't be because of the fool standing in front of her. Count Kushnir wouldn't know what to do with a woman like that if he had a set of instructions and an accompanying magnifying glass.

Rafe let a slow grin curve the corners of his lips, noting the way her eyes widened with alarm as if she too already knew that they were destined to become lovers.

Because they would become lovers. Tonight, tomorrow night—for Rafe it was already a forgone conclusion. He only hoped she wasn't one of those women who liked to play hard to get, imagining that if he had to work for it he'd be more interested. He wouldn't. Because he couldn't be more interested in this woman if he tried.

CHAPTER TWO

ALEXA FELT PRINCE RAFAELE'S gaze on her as if it were a tractor beam.

This was it. The moment she'd been waiting for. The moment he'd notice her so that they would meet and she could introduce herself. Not that she'd probably need to do that because he would surely know who she was but still, it was the polite thing to do. She'd introduce herself, make small talk and…and…

'Choo-choo…choo-choo!'

'I'm sorry?' Forcing her attention back to the man in front of her, with a noble Russian lineage dating back before Peter the Great, she tried to smile. 'I don't think I heard you right?'

At least she hoped she hadn't. But no…there it was again. An obnoxious, high-pitched noise as he mimicked the sound his toy steam engine made as it trundled around an apparently life-sized track. It reminded her of the stories of sybaritic kings of old who set up lifelike warships in large lakes and watched them battle for supremacy. If she had thought this man might be a possible candidate for a fake engagement should Prince Rafaele turn her down, he'd just convinced her to look elsewhere. The only thing she could fake in this man's company was a smile. And even that was growing old.

'May I interrupt?' A smooth deep voice beside her thankfully broke off the man's description of yet another steam engine.

Expecting the voice to belong to Prince Rafaele, she breathed a heavy sigh of relief intermingled with disappointment when it wasn't. Immediately her eyes cut to the place she had last seen him but he wasn't there any more.

'Your Royal Highness?'

Somewhat perplexed that the Prince had simply walked away after staring at her so openly, Alexa smiled at the newcomer beside her. What had he asked her? To dance? 'Yes. Thank you.'

She didn't actually want to dance but maybe movement would help settle her suddenly jangled nerves.

It had been the look the Prince had given her. That all-encompassing male glance that had raked her from head to toe and then pierced her with heat. It had completely thrown her. Of course she'd known he was good-looking. The mouth-watering photos Nasrin had dredged up on the Internet were demonstration enough of that, but in the flesh… In the flesh he was something more. More charismatic. More powerful. More sensual. More *physical*.

Taller than those around him, he'd been wide-shouldered and lean-hipped, his body exuding the kind of animal grace that drew the eye of anyone in his vicinity and held it. His dark brown hair was cut in longer layers, framing his chiselled jaw and well-shaped lips to perfection.

In many ways he'd reminded her of King Jaeger but this man had a laconic, laidback sense to him that was powerfully sexy, and strangely she'd never once thought of the King as sexy.

Powerful, yes. Intimidating and regal, yes. But she'd never looked at him and felt her blood pump faster through her veins, as had happened from one long, wicked look from Prince Rafaele.

Feeling guilty that she was completely ignoring the man who was currently holding her at a respectful distance on the dance floor, she tried to dredge up something interesting to say to break the silence between them. God knew she had years of banal small talk rolling around inside her head but, for the life of her, she couldn't seem to recall any of it, her brain stuck on the strange lethargy that had entered her body at Prince Rafaele's heated stare.

'I hate to cut in, Lord Stanton, but you need

to contact your office. Something about a paternity test being carried out with your name on it.'

'Pardon?' Her dance partner instantly dropped her hand and frowned at the man she'd been waiting all night to 'run into' with horror. 'That can't be true.'

Prince Rafaele gave an indolent shrug of one wide shoulder. 'Don't shoot the messenger.'

Alexa frowned as Lord Stanton mumbled an apology and carved a purposeful path through the crowded dance floor as if the devil was on his trail.

'Allow me,' the Prince said, taking her into his arms and holding her much closer than Lord Stanton had done.

It took her only a moment to realise that he'd done that deliberately, and that there was probably no paternity test in the works at all.

'Was any of that true?'

'Not a word.'

Alexa didn't know whether to laugh or frown at his candour. 'That wasn't very nice. I think you really scared poor Lord Stanton.'

'Only because it's happened to *poor* Lord Stanton before.'

'It has?' She blinked at him. 'How do you know that? Is he a friend of yours?'

'I know everything. But no, he isn't a friend. Not even close.'

'He's not going to be happy when he finds out you lied.'

'Probably not.' The Prince raised an eyebrow as if to say he couldn't care less, his gaze skimming her face. 'But first things first. That soft accent I can hear in your voice isn't French, is it?'

'No.'

'Good.' Before she could think too much about his question he manoeuvred her closer, distracting her. 'Now I can just enjoy how good you feel in my arms.'

Incredibly aware of the warm male chest mere inches from hers, Alexa's breath caught. One of his hard thighs was pressed ever so slightly between her legs, keeping her slightly off balance, so that she had to grip onto his hand to stay upright. Aware that she'd never felt such a powerful response to anyone like this before, she automatically drew back, her reaction causing a slow masculine grin to curve his lips. 'Too fast for you?'

'I...' Completely unprepared to be meeting him like this, let alone be plastered up against his hard body, Alexa frowned. 'Yes. I don't like being crowded.'

Truth be told, she wasn't used to being touched like this. Her father had never been overly tactile and, as her mother had died giving birth to her, she'd been raised by a procession of nannies, each one leaving before she or Sol could become attached to them. It had been her father's way of training any neediness out of them, his methods intended to instil in them both a sense of objectivity and distance befitting a monarch of their realm.

She still remembered the day her beloved Mrs Halstead had left. At five, Alexa had cried herself into a stupor, thus proving her father's point. After a while she had stopped crying when people left but, given the mistake she'd made with Stefano, the lesson in objectivity had taken much longer to master. And sometimes she worried that she still hadn't got it. Especially now, when she was struggling to remain objective in this man's arms.

'By all means I can do slow,' he said with a grin, his mesmerising eyes flicking over her with sensual intent.

Even though she had dressed to attract attention she was so unused to men flirting with her it took Alexa a moment to assimilate his meaning. When she did, heat curved up the side of her neck. She hadn't fully worked out what she was going to say to him when they finally met so she found herself at a loss for words. It was only her love for her country, and a desire to placate her father, that had her still considering going ahead with her plan.

Because ordinarily she wouldn't go near a man

like the Prince. And not just because of his bad
boy reputation but because he was too big and
too male—his level of testosterone swamping
her and making her way too aware of him. It
was like being confronted by an enormous, sated
wolf; even though you knew it was well fed you
still couldn't relax in its presence for fear that it
might pounce just for the fun of it.

The orchestra music changed tempo and she
realised that the Prince danced very well, his
movements fluid and graceful as he moved her
in time with the beat. Wondering how to gain
control of the situation and suggest a place for
them to sit down and talk, she was completely unprepared for his enticing all-male scent to swamp
her as he leaned in closer.

'You're exceptionally beautiful,' he murmured,
bringing her left hand up to his lips in one smooth
move, smiling against her fingertips. 'And un-
married. Two of my favourite attributes in a
woman.'

His earlier question about her being French
came back to her and she pulled back to stare
up at him.

Did he not know who she was?

She'd received so many sympathetic glances
during the night from those who knew her to be
the jilted Princess of Berenia that her teeth had
wanted to grind together.

For him not to recognise her… It didn't seem possible but…perhaps it was. After all, he'd been off doing his own thing for a decade now, where her life had remained incredibly small by comparison. A bolt of inspiration shot through her. If he didn't know who she was it would give her a chance to find out how amenable he would be to her plan without having to embarrass herself by asking outright.

His eyes watched her, confident and direct. Sapphire blue surrounded by inky black lashes, they drew her in with the promise of delights she had probably never even dreamed of, drew her in as if he could read every one of her secret wishes and desires and had the power to answer them all. The notion was both terrifying and utterly irresistible.

The prince's heavy-lidded gaze held an amused glint as if he knew exactly how he was affecting her. Only she didn't plan to become one of his worshippers so it was best to set the scene early.

'Are you always this direct?' she asked, meeting fire with fire.

'I'm not one to waste time on trivialities.' His fingers brushed the inside of her wrist, sending an unexpected trail of goosebumps along her arm. She fought off another tremor as she thought about what those fingers would feel like stroking other, more intimate, parts of her body. 'State what you want and go after it has always been my motto.'

She didn't doubt it.

But ever since her brother had died her life had been mapped out for her and stripped of any real choice so she rarely, if ever, stated what she wanted, or went after it.

He swung her in a tight circle, the hand at the base of her spine covering the small of her back. 'It hasn't failed me yet.' The smile he gave her was one hundred per cent lupine in nature. 'I hope it's not about to.'

'Are you propositioning me?'

The words were out before she could stop them and she only just managed to stop herself from cringing. No doubt none of the sophisticated beauties he was frequently photographed with would need to ask such a gauche question.

Even white teeth were revealed by a frankly amused smile. 'I do believe I am.'

'But you don't even know me.'

'I don't need to know you to know that I want you.' His tone lowered to a sexual purr. 'But if names make you feel more at ease I am Prince Rafaele al-Hadrid. Rafe to my intimates, Rafa to my family.'

'I know who you are,' she said, blinking hard to defuse the sensual spell he was effortlessly weaving around her. 'And I also know of your reputation.'

His smile widened. 'Which one?'

Not sure how to handle the fact that he seemed completely unperturbed by her revelation, Alexa pushed on with her plan to gain information about him. 'The one that says that you're not marriage material.'

'Very true,' he drawled. 'I am good at many things but being a husband would not be one of them. And I believe in playing to my strengths.'

So did she. 'Why wouldn't you be a good husband?'

'According to many of the women I've seen, I'm emotionally stunted, closed off from genuine affection, afraid of true intimacy and utterly self-ish.' His eyes twinkled down at her with amusement. 'I did take exception to the "closed off from genuine affection" comment as I happen to think I'm very affectionate when the mood strikes.'

'I'm sure she was way off base.' Alexa laughed despite herself.

'I'm glad you agree.' He grinned charmingly. 'But you haven't introduced yourself,' he reminded her softly.

'No, I haven't.'

His dark brow arched with quicksilver interest. 'And you're not going to,' he surmised accurately. 'Do you want me to guess?' His gaze roamed her face, heating her up as it went. 'You do seem vaguely familiar. Should I know you?'

'I would say so.'

'Have we ever—'

'No.' She stumbled as his meaning became clear, causing him to bring her into direct contact with his warm body again. Heat that had been simmering away inside her exploded low in her pelvis.

Sensual amusement curved his lips as if he had her right where he wanted her.

Danger, her brain signalled once more, only stronger this time, with the added instruction to retreat. Only she couldn't because she couldn't remember why she should. Not with those intense blue eyes lingering on her lips and turning her mouth so dry she had to fight not to moisten it. Her heart felt like a trapped bird trying to break out of its cage, her whole body assailed with a kind of sweet lethargy she'd never felt before.

The drawn-out notes from a violin signalled the end of the musical score they'd been dancing to, and then someone on the end of a microphone announced that the silent auction was about to take place.

Clusters of murmuring guests started making their way towards one of the anterooms, and Alexa was startled to find that she hadn't moved an inch out of the Prince's arms. Scrambling to get her brain back on line, it took her a moment to realise that he had taken her hand and was leading her in the opposite direction to everyone else.

'Where are you taking me?' She pulled up, digging her spindly heels into the marble floor and gaining no traction at all.

'Somewhere we can talk.' The Prince's enigmatic gaze swept her from head to toe. 'I made a promise that I wouldn't cause any scandals this evening and I'm very close to breaking it.'

He steered her through a set of open doors and along a wide corridor before she had the wherewithal to stop him once more. 'Wait.'

Instantly coming to a halt, he looked back at her.

Alexa blinked as she tried to regulate her thoughts—and her breathing. At some point she would need to get him alone to go over her proposition with him but, with her body sending a whole host of mixed messages to her brain, she knew she wasn't ready for that now. Plus, he wasn't taking her anywhere for them to talk. She might be relatively inexperienced when it came to men, but she already knew that they could be unscrupulous when it came to getting what they wanted.

He looked down at her, amusement lighting his eyes as she gently tugged her hand free of his.

'I'm not going to kiss you.' The bold statement

slipped out before it had fully formed in her mind and she knew she'd never felt as tempted to do exactly what she said she wouldn't in her life before.

His sinful lips curved into that devilish smile and a blush stained her cheeks. 'You don't like kissing?'

Not particularly, but that wasn't the point, was it? 'I don't kiss strangers.'

'But I'm not the stranger here; you are,' he pointed out. 'And fortunately I have no such reservations.'

His tone was teasing but she sensed his hunger in the coiled strength of his body and the heat that radiated from every pore. The earlier image of a wolf about to pounce returned. This time it was definitely hungry and she was in its crosshairs. Rather than scare her as it probably should, it sent another thrill of sensation down her spine. She shuddered with unexpected anticipation and of course he noticed, his blue eyes darkening, his nostrils flaring slightly with his next breath.

Something exciting and wickedly enticing wound between them.

'Come with me,' he invited huskily. 'I get the impression that your life could do with a little excitement in it.'

She wanted to deny it but his assessment was so accurate she couldn't. Every hour of her day was usually accounted for with paperwork or meetings and she rarely took time out to just have fun. A roar of laughter from nearby guests broke into her reverie as if to drive the point home.

Those serious doubts she'd had about going ahead with her plan returned tenfold.

Prince Rafaele was much more lethally male and charismatic than she had anticipated, and the blatantly sexual way he looked at her awoke every one of her senses. She hadn't expected him to have such an uncontrollable edge beneath the civility of his custom-made tuxedo but it was there—primal and dangerous and totally untameable.

'Come,' he coaxed once more, his hand raised towards her. 'Take my hand.'

It was more command than invitation, the silken gravel of his tone making her forget that her future was on the line this weekend. Making her forget how much she had at stake: the ability to fulfil her royal duty to Berenia *her* way.

Against all rational thought, Alexa gave into temptation and placed her hand in his, allowing him to lead her through a solid door and into a beautiful, softly lit reading room. Glancing around, she noted that it was empty, the soft furnishings and gauzy curtains in the windows giving the room an odd sense of intimacy that was heightened when she heard the door click closed behind her.

'I'm not sure this is wise,' she said, knowing by the wild hammering of her heart that it definitely wasn't.

He grinned with mischievous intent. 'Probably not.'

Completely absorbed by the animal grace of his stride as he pushed away from the door and came towards her, Alexa was unprepared for him to invade her personal space and bumped the low table behind her as she unconsciously retreated.

Fortunately, he caught her around the waist, his fingertips spanning her hipbones with blatant possession.

'Your Highness!' Alexa exclaimed on a breathless rush, her mind as unbalanced as her body. 'I told you I'm not—'

'Kissing me. I know.' His head lowered to hers, the warmth of his lips ghosting across the line of her jaw as he inhaled her scent deep into his lungs.

A shiver of awareness bolted down Alexa's spine, turning her knees to water. Her hands flattened against his hard chest as if to hold herself steady, her senses logging the hard heat of his body and the strong beat of his heart through the thick fabric of his jacket.

Despite her four-inch heels, their height difference put her only at eye level with his chiselled mouth and she couldn't look away, her fingers curling of their own accord into his dinner jacket.

The prince's hands firmed on her hips. 'You've got exactly three seconds to step out of my arms before I kiss you properly.'

His tone was low and husky with need and Alexa flushed as an answering need flooded her lower body with silken heat. Completely out of her depth, her knees almost too weak to hold her upright, she leant against him in a move that perfectly signalled her desires to a man well versed in reading the play.

'I'm pretty sure that's five,' he murmured, his head bending as his mouth found hers. This kiss was firm, warm, his lips capturing hers with consummate skill and drawing a response from her she didn't even know she had in her to give.

When she didn't resist a soft groan left his mouth and one of his hands rose to cup the nape of her neck, his body moulding to hers as he took control of her very will.

Alexa knew she shouldn't be doing this but she couldn't seem to organise her thoughts when the desire to taste him was so strong. The prince's heat and scent surrounded her and soaked into her, his mouth driving out any thought of resisting.

'That's it, sweetheart,' he whispered, 'open for me.'

Having never been kissed with such carnal expertise, Alexa felt a rush of burning heat as his tongue entered her mouth and licked at her own. The unexpected eroticism of the move made her hands grip his shoulders, her body arching towards his, seeking more. Craving more.

The sensations were so wickedly enticing that when his fingers curved around one of her breasts she moaned, no longer concerned with what she was here to do. This was all that mattered. This man's mouth fused with hers, his hands caressing her all over and making her burn.

She slid her fingers into his hair, tugging him closer, and he groaned again, his hands moving lower to cup her bottom and bring her in closer against his body, his callused palms snagging on the tiny crystals covering her dress.

'You taste like honey and nectar,' he murmured, his lips trailing a heated line along her jaw towards her ear.

'You taste like heat and mint,' she panted, her neck arching to accommodate his lips, her nipples painfully tight against the fabric of her dress.

He laughed huskily as if she delighted him. It was quite the aphrodisiac after her previous sexual encounter had obliterated her burgeoning self-confidence.

'Come upstairs with me.' The Prince's kisses continued down her neck and she felt him shudder as he gently bit down on the tendons that joined her shoulder. 'I can't take you here; we'll get caught.'

Alexa didn't know which part of that statement permeated her stunned senses more, but suddenly her hands were firm on the hard balls of his biceps as she pushed him back. Memories of her teenage mistake tumbled into the space between them, tripping up her thoughts as she fought to draw oxygen into her lungs and clear the haze from her brain. 'We can't... I'm not... Let me go!'

As soon as the words were out he released her, his chest heaving like bellows as his breath rasped in and out of his lungs.

His dark hair was in disarray around his shoulders and she realised with a mortified groan that her fingers must have done that.

'What's wrong?'

'What's wrong?' Her eyes widened at his ridiculous question. 'We nearly... I just... I didn't come in here for that.'

Struggling to even out his breathing as much as she was, the Prince's brows drew together. 'Why did you come in here then?'

Still experiencing the drugging after-effects of being in his arms, Alexa blurted out the first thing that came into her head. 'I came in here to ask you to marry me.'

CHAPTER THREE

'You SHOULD HAVE gone with that as your opening line, sweetheart,' Prince Rafaele drawled. 'It would have smothered the chemistry between us faster than a Santarian sandstorm.'

Unsure how to handle him as well as her rioting emotions, Alexa frowned. 'I didn't expect you to pounce on me as soon as we got here.'

'Pounce?' He gave an amused look. 'I gave you a chance to pull back.'

'Three seconds?'

His grin deepened. 'It ended up being five.'

'You don't even know my name,' she said, flabbergasted that he could so quickly switch from arousal to amusement when she was still struggling for composure.

'I've never found that to be all that important when I want a woman.'

Well, that stung. No woman wanted to be just another notch on a man's bedpost. But what had she expected? This was the exalted Rebel Prince who had attempted to seduce her. Attempted and nearly succeeded! 'Why?' she felt compelled to ask. 'Because you don't plan on seeing the woman again?' she challenged.

'Now that depends on the night. And the woman.' His eyes narrowed on her face as if he was trying to work something out. 'So who are you? Because I have to admit you're damned familiar, although I know I've never touched you before.'

She didn't know whether to be flattered by that statement or not and went with not. 'My name is Alexa, Crown Princess of the House of Berenia.' She gave her tone just the right amount of haughtiness to signal her displeasure with him, and was pleased when his eyes widened.

He raked a hand through his hair. 'You might have mentioned that sooner as well.'

'I did plan to when we got inside the room, but you kissed me before I could come out with it.'

Rafe's gaze dropped to her lips and he cursed under his breath. She was right. He'd never acted on his attraction for a woman faster. His only excuse being that he'd felt her hunger run as deep as his own and he'd been unable to resist testing that hunger when they were alone. And he'd been right. She'd gone off like a firecracker in his arms. Another few minutes and they both would have been naked and horizontal.

Thank God he'd had enough sense to suggest they go to his room, and the restraint to release her when she'd asked. But he hadn't wanted to. The inferno that she had lit inside him had been ready to explode. It still was, but this time partly with recrimination. He should probably apologise for pouncing on her as she had accused him of doing. It wasn't his usual style, which leant itself to more finesse and a small measure of self-control!

And she was his brother's cast-off, dammit, the daughter of the man who was currently making his brother's life hell. Jag would just love it if he had witnessed this near blunder. It had been one thing to piss his father off deliberately, but he'd never do that to his brother.

'Well, I'm not kissing you now, Princess, so I suggest we leave and forget this ever happened.'

If he could. He had a feeling he'd be dreaming about the taste of her mouth and those soft kittenish sounds she'd made as he'd cupped her bottom in his hands for a few nights yet. Even now he wanted to reach for her again.

'But I was serious about what I said before.' She drew in a long breath, her lovely breasts straining against the fabric of her gown. 'And I'd really like to make a time to speak with you about it.'

Rafe sent his mind back and focused on what

she'd said that had halted him in his tracks. 'Marriage?'

'Well, engaged more than married.'

He shook his head gently, unable to believe that she was actually serious. 'I don't do marriage. You'll have to find someone else to fulfil that fantasy.'

'I know you don't do marriage. That's the point. I don't either.'

He frowned at her earnest expression. She was either crazy or… 'How much have you had to drink, Princess, because you're not making any sense?'

'I've hardly had anything to drink,' she retorted as if he'd insulted her. 'I'm perfectly sober.'

'Then that response before was all you?' He gave her a lazy smile as her cheeks coloured. 'Good to know.'

'I'd rather not talk about that.' Her lips pinched together. 'And, given what just happened, now probably isn't the best time to discuss my proposal. Could we meet tomorrow?'

'Tomorrow isn't going to change my mind. Neither will the day after.'

'Look…' she held her hands up as if to placate him '… I'm not talking about a real marriage. I'm talking about a temporary engagement that works for us both. We won't even have to spend that much time together. We just need to put out a joint statement, go to a couple of events together and break up amicably at a time that suits us both.'

'As far as proposals go, this one is definitely novel, but marriage—sorry, *engagement*—doesn't work for me at all. Temporary or not.'

'I know.' She gave a heavy sigh, tucking a strand of thick silky hair that had come loose back behind her ear. She looked gloriously mussed from where his hands had been and that reminded him of how much he'd like to put them there again. Unwind all that magnificent hair and find out how long it was.

As if they had a will of their own, his eyes followed her as she paced the mahogany-decked reading room, her gown hugging her heavenly curves as she moved. 'That's why I chose you.'

'Chose me?' He blinked to get his brain back on line.

'Yes,' she said with the patience of a mother speaking to a recalcitrant child. 'I need to get married—or at least engaged—and you have all the attributes I want in a fiancé.'

Curious, Rafe found himself extending the conversation, if only for the amusement factor. 'Such as?'

'You follow your own rules, you're completely disinterested in marriage, and your values in life are questionable.'

'Questionable?'

'According to everything that's said about you, you're quite the hedonist.'

Rafe leant against the back of a sofa. 'Really?'

'I'm paraphrasing. But the point is we're completely incompatible so it won't surprise anyone when we don't go through with the marriage, and no one will be blamed for it not working out.' Unlike when his brother had called off their engagement and everyone had thought it was her fault. That she hadn't been woman enough for the King of Santara. 'It will just seem obvious.'

'I have to confess,' Rafe drawled, 'I've never had those reasons put forward by a woman wanting me to put a ring on her finger before. Usually it's more along the lines of: *You're rich, powerful and a prince.*'

'Oh, the prince part is important to me too. At least that you're from Santara.' She frowned as she perched on the edge of the sofa. 'Women actually say that to you?'

'I was paraphrasing.' His eyes glinted mockingly. 'So why is my being a Santarian prince important to you? I would have thought it was the last thing you would want.'

'My father is convinced that seeing me happily settled will ease the current tension between Santara and Berenia and help our people move forward from your brother breaking our betrothal. He gave me six months to find someone, but I didn't realise he was serious. Now he's planning to take matters into his own hands and arrange a marriage that I don't want.'

'Ah, I'm beginning to see the picture.'

She let out a slow breath, her narrow shoulders slumping slightly forward. 'When my father is like this he's immovable, and I need more time.'

'Hmm…' Feeling a little sorry for her, Rafe offered up the only solution he could think of. 'You know you could always say no.'

'No isn't a word my father understands.'

'Is doormat a word *you* understand?'

Her eyes flashed up at him like deep pools of jade backlit by fire. 'Are you implying that I'm a doormat?'

Rafe shrugged, enjoying her display of defiance. 'If the shoe fits.'

'The shoe does not fit,' she said a little too vehemently. 'The fact is my father has been through a lot in recent years and I'm not going to add to his problems. And this is partly your brother's fault. If he had gone ahead with our marriage as he had agreed to do then none of this would be an issue right now.'

'But nor would you have got to kiss me quite so passionately, so there is that.'

Her feathers well and truly ruffled, the Princess pushed to her feet. 'You either have a colossal ego or you're making fun of me.'

'Let's go with the ego theory. A lot less volatile.' Rafe crossed to the booze cabinet between two arched bookcases and poured himself a whisky. 'Drink?' he asked, holding the crystal decanter up for her to see.

She set her top teeth into her plush bottom lip, reminding him of how exquisite her mouth had felt under his, and surprised him with a terse nod.

'Dutiful does not equal doormat, you know.' She moved towards him, careful not to touch his fingers as she took the glass. He gave her a small smile that said he knew exactly how nervous he made her and watched her chin come up in response. 'Not that I expect you to understand that.'

'I understand it,' he said curtly. 'I just don't adhere to it.'

'Well, you're lucky. I don't have that choice.'

Rafe clinked the ice in his glass, wondering what it was about her he found so enthralling. Because he did find her enthralling—from the way she moved to the feminine lilt in her voice, and definitely in the sexy lines of her body. He suspected that she took life far too seriously, and for some reason he wanted to change that.

'You're an intelligent, beautiful woman,' he

began, watching her closely. 'And a future queen. How hard can it be to find a husband?'

'It's not hard at all.' She sighed. 'But finding the *right* husband is.'

'Do I even want to know what the right husband looks like?'

'Someone kind, compassionate, caring.' She took a delicate sip of his brother's hundred-year-old Scotch, shuddering delicately as it hit the back of her throat. 'Someone I can respect and who will put Berenia first. Someone who has a similar outlook to me.'

'Not looking for someone with a sense of humour?' he enquired lightly.

Alexa frowned. 'That would go under "similar outlook to me".'

'So none then.' He grinned as her eyes widened. 'What about love?'

'I have a sense of humour, thank you very much,' she defended hotly. 'And love is not essential.'

Rafe's eyes widened at that. 'I think you're the first woman I've ever heard admit that.'

'Love complicates things and who even knows if it exists? I think it's made up by Hollywood executives and songwriters trying to make money.'

'And I thought I was cynical.' Her brow furrowed and his grin widened. 'That was a compliment, by the way. But what about passion? Surely that's on your list.'

She wrinkled her nose. 'Not essential either. I'm not the most passionate person on the planet, and respect far outweighs passion.'

Contemplating what had put her off passion when his body still throbbed at the memory of her mouth opening under his, Rafe gave her a smile that was pure sex. 'You felt pretty passionate to me before.'

She moved to sit again on the sofa, unable to meet his gaze. 'That wasn't me. I don't know who that person was.'

'Whoever she was, she was intoxicating.'

She wrinkled her nose. 'So will you consider it? I'm not sure how long I have before my father takes the decision completely out of my hands. And, frankly, I'm desperate.'

'I can see that.' He was actually sorry he had to turn her offer down. If life hadn't taught him that he needed to steer clear of matrimonial entanglements at all costs he might even have considered it. But marriage had the potential to inflict pain on the unwary and the innocent. Why would any man deliberately buy into that? Temporary or not. 'Sorry, Princess, but I'm not that desperate.'

'You won't even consider it to help improve relations between our nations?'

Rafe blinked away the dark memories of his past and found himself pinned by a pair of gorgeous green eyes that, if he wasn't careful, had the potential to suck him in deep and never let him go. 'See, the problem with that part of your argument is that I don't care about the issues between Santara and Berenia.'

She blinked as if he'd just said *Down with world peace*. 'But how can you not?'

'I live in London and have done for a decade. I have as little to do with Santara as I can.'

'Then what about to improve your reputation? Being engaged to me would stop some of the gossip. For a while at least.'

Princess Alexa, he realised, was a real fighter. He liked that. Not enough to agree with her harebrained scheme, but enough to find that he was enjoying her company. A lot.

'Who said I wanted the gossip to stop?'

'But surely some of the things written about you must bother you.'

'Not particularly.'

'Why is that?' Her brow pleated as if his attitude was something she couldn't contemplate. 'Because it's all true?'

Rafe wondered which particular piece of gossip had widened her eyes to the size of dinner plates. Hardly any of it was true but denying the many claims made about him would only give them energy so he rarely bothered. Still, he knew that Alexa didn't think much of his supposedly 'hedonistic' lifestyle and he couldn't help teasing her a little. 'Only the really bad ones.'

Watching the wings of colour heat her cheeks almost made him want to rescind his words so that she'd think better of him. Then he wondered why he cared and remained silent. He didn't like that he'd already delayed this conversation for the pure pleasure of listening to her speak. Adding to his uncharacteristic behaviour would only make things worse.

'So your answer is no?'

'My answer is no.'

She blew out a breath and set her glass on the table abutting the sofa. 'Then there's nothing more to say.'

There was plenty more to say, starting with enquiring which room she had been allocated so they could revisit that kiss, the sensations of which were still echoing inside his veins. But instead he said, 'What are you going to do now?'

She raised her chin and gave him a look he imagined she gave international dignitaries she had no further use for. 'Find someone else, of course.'

Find someone else? Rafe scowled at his fogged-up reflection as he stepped from the shower the following morning. *Just how many men did she plan to approach with her absurd proposal? And, more importantly, had she found someone who had taken her up on her offer last night?*

He didn't want that question running through his head but he was unable to banish it. After she had walked away from him he'd spent another hour at the party looking for her, to no avail. Presumably she'd gone to bed, so he had done the same, thinking about her all night as he'd known he would.

Even though he had no intention of countenancing her proposal himself, he knew that someone would eventually agree to it. What sane man wouldn't? With that face and body…

Rafe dropped his towel on the floor and padded back to his room to dress. *He'd* turned her down, hadn't he, and he was a sane man.

Yes, but he was sane and *smart*. Smart enough to know that her problems were none of his business and that he should let it go.

And he would. As of now.

His jet was waiting to fly him back to London and he planned to stop downstairs long enough to grab an espresso, wish his sister-in-law well in her pregnancy and tell his siblings he'd see them some time in the future.

What he wouldn't do was think about the beguiling Alexa any more today.

Pleased to be back on track, he pulled a clean shirt over his head, stepped into his jeans and shoved his feet into his boots.

Women just shouldn't go around proposing to men who were basically strangers and expect that it would all work out exactly as they wanted it to. Especially not future queens who looked like cover girls. Alexa was asking for trouble.

Trouble that had nothing to do with him.

And why was she back in his head again? So she'd surprised him when so few people did any more—so what? At the end of the day she was just a beautiful woman he'd wanted to take to bed. And she'd wanted to be there too. The way she'd caught fire in his arms…her response to his touch… Grinding his teeth, he zipped his overnight bag closed. What she'd done was drive all rational thought from his head, and kept him up way too long last night.

But it wasn't just the chemistry that had kept him awake. It was the puzzle she represented. She'd gone up like a flame in his arms but then claimed that she didn't have a passionate nature, dismissing the desire between them as an anomaly. And what about her belief that love might not exist? Presumably something, or someone, had put that in her head and he'd like to know who or what. Not that he disagreed with her. He didn't. He didn't believe in love either, but something about the way she'd said it made him think that she was either lying to him, or lying to herself. And yet she'd seemed so honest…so sincere…

Scowling at the procession of questions that wouldn't say die, Rafe grabbed his phone. Time to push Princess Alexa from his mind and think about something else. Because thinking about her made no sense. She wasn't someone he planned to pursue—not with marriage on her mind—and added to that she was his brother's ex, for God's sake.

Assailed by a sudden wave of jealousy he'd never before felt for his brother, Rafe nearly put a hole in his pocket shoving his phone into it. He didn't share his women. Ever.

And since when is a woman yours after one kiss?

Leaving that ridiculous question unanswered, he slammed out of his room and made his way to breakfast. He needed coffee before his mood deteriorated any further.

Refusing to wonder if he'd meet up with the beguiling Alexa, he heard a message arrive on his phone and homed in on it like a drowning man reaching for a life vest. Unfortunately, it was only a stock commodity update and he was in the process of closing it when he nearly barrelled into Jag as he rounded the corner of his private hallway.

Instantly alerted by his brother's taut, exhausted expression, Rafe frowned. 'What is it? Is there something wrong with Regan?'

Rafe might not have much to do with his brother any more but he could still read him and he couldn't think of anything else that might put that ragged look on his brother's face other than his wife, or all-out war.

'No, Regan's fine. I've just come from a meeting with King Ronan and Princess Alexa.'

Rafe felt himself instantly tense. 'They haven't declared war, have they?'

'Not yet.' Jag's scowl deepened. 'But last night a firebomb was thrown into a building site near the border in a show of protest at King Ronan and Princess Alexa attending the charity ball last night. Two of our workers were injured.'

'That's insane,' Rafe growled. 'Why did the King even attend if things are that volatile?'

'We believed it would be a display of unity between us but the Berenians didn't take it that way. They see my slight of their Princess as the highest insult.' He smiled faintly. 'Sorry to burden you with my problems. It was nice seeing you mucking around with Milena. It's a pity we don't see each other more often. I know Regan would like it if we did. I would too.'

Rafe swallowed the lump that suddenly lodged in his throat. He loved his siblings but he wasn't like either of them; he was a loner. He didn't require the same level of closeness, or connection, that drove others to forge unbreakable bonds. He didn't need someone, or something, special and neither Jag nor Milena understood that about him.

'Let's focus on one thing at a time. What can I do to help sort out the Berenia thing?'

Alexa's proposal of the previous night came into his head and he instantly shelved it. Marriage—or becoming engaged—was not the answer here.

'I thought you needed to head back to London?'

'I do. But if there's something I can assist you with while I'm here then I will. I'm not so obtuse that I can't see how much you have on your plate right now.' Not that he expected that Jag would need him. Their father never had. The important issues he'd gone to Jag for counsel. Rafe had been relegated to the lesser duties of opening flower shows or attending state dinners where he was expected to be on his best behaviour to prove what a great parent and leader his father was. Rafe was pretty sure they hadn't fooled anyone on that score.

'I appreciate the offer but, as I said, I've just had a meeting with King Ronan and Princess Alexa. We've come up with a diplomatic response to ease the tension.'

Rafe had a feeling he wasn't going to like the response. 'What was decided?'

'You really want to know?'

Yes, for once he really did.

'Why not? I'm here and I am still a Santarian.'

'Princess Alexa has agreed to a union with Lord Alec Richton of Urbana. I'm not sure when the wedding will take place, but the plan is for Lord Richton to fly into Berenia later in the week for a formal announcement.'

Rafe's whole body went still. 'You've got to be kidding me?'

'No, why would I do that?'

'Because it's barbaric and I can't believe you'd allow Alexa to be bandied around like a box of chocolates everyone can take a pick at.'

Jag frowned at his harsh tone. 'That's hardly what's happening here.'

'Isn't it?' Rafe felt unreasonably livid. 'You were betrothed to her.'

'When King Ronan approached me early last year I said I'd consider the idea,' Jag said evenly. 'It was never a done deal, and it should not have been made public.'

'So now Richton gets a go at her?' Rafe swore under his breath. 'What if he pulls out? Do you and Ronan have someone else up your sleeve for her?'

Jag's gaze sharpened. 'Someone else…?' His

tone turned thoughtful. 'That's the kind of question a jealous lover might ask.'

'Hardly.' Unable to remain still under his brother's perceptive gaze, Rafe paced the floor.

'Richton won't pull out,' Jag said. 'Apparently he's been in talks with King Ronan for some months about a union, but regardless, the Princess is an incredibly lovely and intelligent woman. Most men would jump at the chance to marry her.'

Rafe knew how lovely she was, and having his brother notice only made his aggravation deepen. 'But what about what she wants?'

Jag sighed. 'I really don't understand what's got you so het-up about this but she does want it. We all want to end the hostilities between Berenia and Santara so we can move forward. If Alexa's marriage is able to promote peace in the minds of the Berenians, then I'm all for it.' He frowned as Rafe continued to pace. 'Come on, Rafa. You know that arranged marriages have been happening here for centuries. They've worked out in the past, and they'll work for a while to come yet.'

Too agitated to argue with his brother any further, Rafe headed for the door. 'We'll see,' he said, slamming it closed behind him.

He found Alexa in the breakfast room, speaking to another of the guests who had stayed overnight at the palace.

The smell of coffee made his saliva glands go into overdrive but he bypassed the silver pot on the sideboard and headed straight for Alexa.

As he neared he realised she was speaking to Lord Graham, the son of an English earl. Had he been another one of her candidates?

Not that it mattered any more.

'Princess Alexa?' He stopped beside her, completely ignoring Lord Graham. 'We need to talk.'

Clearly startled by his abrupt tone, her green eyes widened. 'Your Highness?'

'I told you last night, it's Rafe. I rarely use my title.'

'Prince Rafaele…' Lord Graham frowned at him. 'Princess Alexa and I are in the middle of—'

'Nothing.' Rafe turned his most cutting gaze on Graham. He knew he could be intimidating; he owned nightclubs and had been called upon to throw more than one drunken patron out onto the pavement, so he wasn't surprised when the other man's eyes flickered warily. 'The Princess and I have…unfinished business to settle.'

Not at all as intimidated by him as Graham, Alexa frowned. 'What unfinished business?'

Unprepared to stand around explaining himself in the middle of a room full of people, Rafe raised a brow. 'Have you forgotten the proposal you made last night? Perhaps you were drunk after all.'

'I was not!'

'Then you haven't forgotten.' He cut his gaze back to Graham, who had foolishly remained rooted to the spot. 'And unless you want Lord Graham here to be privy to our chat I suggest we take this somewhere private.'

Clearly unimpressed with his high-handed tactics, Alexa's mouth tightened. 'Fine. Please accept my apologies, Lord Graham. Prince Rafaele obviously has a bee in his bonnet about something.'

A bee in his bonnet?

Rafe shook his head and reached for her elbow. 'You don't have to be nice to everyone, you know. Graham will survive without your company for a while.'

Rafe directed Alexa through a nearby door to a small private terrace, which was thankfully empty.

'You need to stop doing that,' she complained, glaring up at him. 'I am not a horse to be led around at will.'

She brushed past him as she moved out of the direct line of the sun and the subtle scent of her perfume drew his muscles tight.

Irritated that he was affected by a woman who wasn't even trying to win his favour, Rafe met her icy stare with one of his own. 'All evidence to the contrary.'

'What does that mean?'

'It means I've just spoken with my brother, who informed me about your impending nuptials with Lord Richton.'

'He had no right to do that.'

'Why not? He didn't reveal anything I wouldn't know in a week or two anyway.'

'Then you also know why we reached the decision.'

'Because a group of hot-headed Berenians went about a hundred steps too far? Yes, I heard. Did you ever think of just calling in the army for protection?'

'Oh, that would really work,' she scoffed. 'Make a show of aggression and give the BLF even more of an excuse to start a war. Maybe you could lend us a few of the bouncers who work the doors at your nightclubs for extra muscle.'

'It seems a damn sight better than marrying someone to reach an outcome it might not even achieve.'

Her eyes narrowed at his disparaging comment. 'Diplomacy is always better than might.'

Not in his view. 'I take it this marriage isn't of the fake variety,' he said, an edge in his voice he was struggling to control.

'No.' She paused, as if what she was about to

say was distasteful, staring out over the expanse of green lawn surrounded by potted roses and gardenia bushes. 'It won't be fake.'

Silent fury made his voice gruff. 'Is that what you want? To marry Richton?'

She gave him a fulminating look. 'You know it isn't.'

'But you'll do it anyway.'

'If my country needs me to do it.' Her chin lifted, as if daring him to contradict her. 'Then yes, I'll do it.'

'The dutiful little mouse.'

Jade fire flashed from her eyes at his mocking tone but what did she expect, that he'd ignore the obvious?

'I am no more a mouse than a doormat,' she said icily.

'You're doing something you don't want to do. I'd say that makes you one or the other.'

'Sometimes sacrifices have to be made,' she said with regal fortitude. 'Why do you care?'

'I don't like injustice. And I know how it feels to be trapped by circumstance.' He knew how it felt to be bullied into doing something you didn't want to do. His father had made an art form out of it, and it seemed her father was doing the same to her. 'It's why I left Santara.'

'So you're trying to help me? Very chivalrous, Prince Rafaele,' she mocked softly. 'But I don't have the luxury of choice. I have to marry at some point.' She swallowed heavily and turned her gaze out over the elaborate garden once more. 'It might as well be Lord Richton.'

Watching how controlled and closed-up she was only made Rafe's temper hit a new high. 'Richton might seem like an upstanding citizen, but word is that he has a dark side. One you don't want to meet.'

'How would you know that?'

'Because he's been blacklisted from at least seven clubs that I'm aware of, including mine.'

A grimace crossed her face as she shook her head. 'I'd prefer not to know that.'

'Dammit, Alexa. That's not even the point here.' He stepped closer, deliberately crowding her. 'Stop being a martyr.'

'My, you have a lot of names for me, don't you?' she mocked, her eyes cool enough to freeze lava.

Yes, he did have a lot of names for her, utterly beautiful being one of them.

'My brother died three years ago,' she said, a note of sadness replacing the iciness of moments ago, 'leaving all of us utterly devastated and me the only heir to the throne. When you add in the problems with Santara, combined with the corruption my father has just weeded out of our government, that has set back our modernisation plans and given the BLF even more to gripe about, you can see that something has to be done. And quickly.'

'I'm sorry you lost your brother, and I'm sorry you're facing political challenges, but that doesn't mean you just give up.'

'I'm not a quitter!' she denied hotly. 'I'm not giving up. I'm giving in. There's a difference.'

'I don't see that.'

'You don't have to. And I'm sorry if asking you to marry me last night made you think that you have the right to question me. In hindsight, the whole fake engagement idea was a mistake. It probably wouldn't have worked anyway. I was desperate for an alternative but now I don't need one. If by marrying Lord Richton I can ease the political tension between our two countries, and prevent more violence, then I'll consider that a win.'

He saw the line of her throat move as she swallowed. She was putting on a brave face but he'd bet that she wanted to marry Richton about as much as a person wanted a root canal. She was just too nice to say it. Too nice to demand her due. And that bothered him. Almost as much as it bothered him to imagine Alec Richton putting his hands on her. His mouth.

'Have you even met Richton?' he grated.

'Of course.'

'Have you kissed him?'

'That's none of your business.'

It wasn't difficult to read that she was furious with his question. As she had a right to be. He was behaving entirely out of character, getting involved with a woman beyond the bedroom, especially with a woman he had already made off-limits. He didn't bed women who were looking for marriage—either temporary or permanent. Especially not princesses from politically hostile neighbouring countries.

And yet thinking of her married to some other man when she'd kissed him as she had the night before left a nasty taste in his mouth. And that was strange in itself. He'd kissed—hell, he'd made love to—plenty of women and never given a thought to who they might end up with. The notion had never entered his head before.

But then he'd never been as attracted to a woman as he was to this one. It was something he wasn't sure how to handle. Because he still wanted her. In fact right now he wanted to take her into his arms, press her back against the wall and challenge her to ignore the sexual chemistry that pulsed between them.

'I'm making it my business,' he said, noting how her eyes widened at his tone.

'You can't.' She made to move past him and her body brushed his. Raw, unparalleled desire arced between them, making a mockery of her words. Frowning in consternation, he knew she would have put more space between them if she hadn't found herself neatly trapped between him and an outdoor table. 'Marriages in our part of the world have been arranged for centuries,' she continued, raising irritated eyes to his. 'It's a tradition.'

'That's what my brother said. But I'm a bit of an anti-traditionalist unless both parties are in agreement.'

'Not all of us have the freedom that you do. And I have a duty to uphold.'

'A duty that will lead you into a worse situation than you're already in.'

'That's your opinion, not mine. An opinion you have no right to offer since you very clearly turned down my proposal last night.'

'And the chemistry between us?' He hadn't realised he'd moved closer to her until she made to move away from him again. Irritated, he reached out and clasped her wrist in his hand. It was fine-boned, delicate, so small. His body hardened as memories of how she had felt in his arms coursed through his veins. Of how her nails had dug into his shoulders through his clothing. He wanted that again, but directly on his skin this time. 'You're just going to walk away from it? You're going to pretend that you didn't dream about me last night?'

Her breath left her in a soft rush. 'I did not dream about you last night.'

'I dreamt about you.'

Her eyes widened at the admission, her sharp inhalation setting every one of his nerve-endings on fire.

'What would you have me do?' She shot him a wary look, as well she might, given the nature of the questions and the answering thoughts currently running through his head.

What a pity that he couldn't give into any of them.

'I'd have you stand up for what you want,' he bit out. Which was true enough. Being dutiful was one thing, being foolish another thing entirely.

She shook her head as if that wasn't even a possibility. 'Sometimes the only way to win is to retreat. It's called strategy.'

'It's called insanity.'

'To you,' she said curtly. 'To me it's my duty. But I still don't understand why you're so interested in all this. Apart from wanting to play the white knight, that is.'

'I don't play the white knight,' Rafe growled. He'd done that as a boy, stepping in between his parents during their more vitriolic arguments to protect his mother from his father's rages. Neither parent had appreciated the conciliatory gesture—his father thinking him insubordinate, and therefore worthless, and his mother too caught up in her own pain to notice his.

The memory was a timely reminder as to why he steered clear of emotional entanglements. Entanglements like this.

'And you're right. This isn't my business. If you want to marry Richton and commit to a life of unhappiness then have it.'

'I didn't say I *wanted* that.'

'Then what do you want?'

Already charged with emotions he was unused to feeling, Rafe's jaw clenched. She must have read his tension accurately because her gaze dropped to his mouth, her tongue darting out to moisten her lips. The air between them went from volatile to explosive. The pulse in her neck throbbed and her eyes widened as if she sensed danger. But she didn't move away.

Instead she went still, her whole body taut as if she was waiting for something. As if she was *wanting* something...

Rafe told himself not to do it. Not to reach for her. Not to touch her. But he might as well have told himself to cut off his own foot while he was at it.

'Ah, to hell with it.' Without giving either of

them a chance to think, and completely disregarding any consequences, Rafe lowered his mouth to hers.

If she'd shown any form or resistance or hesitation he might have stopped, he might have pulled back and reminded himself that she was not only 'off-limits', but that he didn't go around kissing women just to prove a point. But she didn't resist. Instead she gave a low moan of assent, wound her arms around his neck and pulled him in closer.

This. *This* was what he'd woken up craving today. The soft velvet feel of her mouth under his again, the sweet taste of her on his tongue and the long length of her warm curves moulded to the hard planes of his body.

Shock waves of pleasure shot through him as her fingers gripped his hair, her tongue caressing along his, filling his mouth as she shyly tasted him in return. Rafe groaned, curving his fingers around the slender nape of her neck, his thumbs firm against her cheeks as he deepened the kiss. He couldn't seem to get enough of her. Her taste, her touch. He wanted more, he needed—

'What the devil is the meaning of this?'

Rafe knew instantly that the deep voice that thundered behind Alexa was her father, and from the way her body instantly stiffened so did she.

He could have kicked himself. Never before had he become so lost in a woman, so lost in his own senses, that he'd forgotten his surroundings the way he just had. The way he nearly had the night before.

Cursing softly, he raised his head to see the shocked fury on her father's face, followed by the shocked disbelief on his brother's.

Alexa's stricken gaze rose to his. 'Please tell me it's not as bad as I think,' she whispered un-evenly.

'Worse,' he murmured, his gaze firmly fixed on her father.

'Well? Are you just going to stand there and ignore me?' the King thundered. 'I want to know the meaning of this! Alexa? Explain yourself.'

Straightening her shoulders, Alexa moistened her kiss-swollen lips and turned to face her father's wrath, smoothing her hands down over her hips. 'Father… Your Majesty…' Her face flamed anew as her gaze landed on his brother, a fresh wave of mortification turning her cheeks rosy. 'I was… That is to say we were…'

'Celebrating,' Rafe said, knowing that there was only one way out of this mess and taking it.

'Celebrating?' King Ronan's face became almost mottled.

'Rafe—' Alexa's worried gaze met his as if

she had already guessed what he was about to say, but Rafe ignored the look.

Taking her hand in his, he raised it to his lips. 'That's right,' he confirmed, his eyes never leaving hers. 'Alexa and I were celebrating our betrothal.'

CHAPTER FOUR

'BETROTHAL?'

Her father's voice was imbued with such a note of incredulity that Alexa knew immediately what he was thinking—that this man would never do as her future consort. It was only Rafe's rank as second in line to the throne of Santara that kept complete scorn from his voice.

'That's right,' the Prince drawled lazily.

Alexa nearly groaned out loud at the Prince's antagonistic tone.

'Is this true, Alexa?' Her father's voice sliced like a filleting knife. 'Did you accept Prince Rafaele's hand in marriage?'

No, *she* had asked *him*. And he'd said no. But, that aside, how was she to answer his question diplomatically when she had no idea *how* to answer it at all? Rafe had thrown her in at the deep end with his charged announcement and she wasn't at all sure why he had done it. An outright denial seemed implausible given that she'd been caught with her arms wrapped around the

Prince like a vine, but agreeing seemed just as problematic.

Fortunately her father was too incensed to notice that she was struggling to come up with an answer and didn't have the patience for her to formulate one. 'After we had already agreed that you would marry Lord Richton this morning?'

Oh, dear. Lord Richton. She had completely forgotten about him. If the floor were to open up and swallow her whole right now, she wouldn't mind.

'Lord Richton is no longer in the picture,' the Prince declared, his hard-packed body lethally tense beside her.

Alexa frowned at the way he took control of the situation, at the way he took control of her, as if he had every right to do so.

Just then a flutter of movement caught her eye and Alexa was appalled to note that they were no longer alone. Some of the King's other overnight guests had also come out to the terrace to view the stunning gardens.

'Why don't we take this discussion inside?' King Jaeger offered smoothly. 'The terrace is hardly the place to discuss something of this magnitude.'

Her father looked like he wanted to argue but gave a curt nod.

Rafe settled his hand in the small of her

back, causing a jolt of fresh awareness to race through her.

'After you,' he said politely.

Hanging back from her father and his brother, Alexa glanced up at him from beneath the fringe of her lashes. 'Why on earth did you tell them we were betrothed?' she whispered hoarsely, absently noting that Rafe had matched his stride to hers.

'Because I could hardly tell your father that I wanted to take you to bed, and that you wanted to be there. I do value my life,' he countered.

Not nearly enough, she fumed silently at his cavalier answer.

'Just because I kissed you does not mean that I want to sleep with you!' she hissed, wondering if she would have had the wherewithal to deny him this time if it had come to that.

'My apologies, Princess. I assumed you wouldn't want a scandal any more than I do, and you did ask me to marry you. I thought it was what you wanted.'

It had been. Last night. Last night, before he had kissed her and brought forth a whole host of emotions she didn't want to feel. Before she had dreamt about the two of them in bed together. Naked.

Easing out a choked breath, Alexa nodded at King Jaeger as he held a door open. She reluctantly followed her father inside, with Rafe so close behind her she could feel his body heat through her clothing.

At least she understood his thinking now. He'd promised his brother that he wouldn't create a scandal and so he'd improvised by taking up her proposal. Something she should feel much better about, given that it *was* her idea and it *had* been what she wanted.

Only the purpose of asking the Prince to marry her was to *gain* control of her life, and she somehow felt that she was about to lose it altogether.

She surreptitiously placed a finger against her temple, which had started to throb. She supposed there was no other option but to go along with it now because Rafe was right; she didn't want to marry Lord Richton, and she had always viewed a fake engagement as a better option.

King Jaeger offered her father a seat but he refused, choosing to stand beside an oak dresser, his arms folded across his corpulent chest.

Rafe planted himself in the middle of the room, his legs braced wide on the silk rug, facing his brother. Not wanting to be the only person in the room seated, Alexa chose to remain beside him, even though her legs felt as capable of holding her up as matchsticks.

'Well, now that we're all standing,' King Jaeger

began with a resigned note in his voice, 'would someone mind explaining what's going on here?'

'There's nothing to explain,' Rafe began. 'Alexa and I share a certain *chemistry*, and have decided to take things further.'

Wondering why he hadn't led with the political advantages their union would bring, Alexa was only grateful that he hadn't chosen to reveal how she had approached him the night before.

'When did this happen?' her father asked suspiciously.

'We spoke about it last night,' Rafe answered, throwing her a heated glance that told her exactly which part of last night he was thinking about. 'At length.'

'If you spoke about it last night, Alexa—' her father's gaze pierced hers '—why did you agree to marry Lord Richton during the meeting this morning?'

'Last night I got cold feet,' Rafe interjected smoothly, placing his arm around her waist. 'It put Alexa in an awkward position. After thinking things through however, I now know what I want. Do you think we could ring for coffee? I'm parched.'

'I was addressing my daughter,' her father snapped impatiently. 'Alexa can speak for herself.'

Yes, but nowhere near as eloquently. She was

almost in awe of how the Prince could reveal so much and yet so little at the same time.

'Prince Rafaele is correct, Father,' she said, trying to ignore the heavy warmth of Rafe's hand against her hip. 'We did speak about it last night and I'm… I'm still coming to terms with his change of heart.' She glanced at the Prince with a look just short of panic, hoping that King Jaeger had indeed rung for coffee—or perhaps something stronger.

'Sometimes a man doesn't know what's important until it's about to be taken away.' Prince Rafaele gave her an indulgent smile. 'When Alexa informed me of your plan to marry her off to Lord Richton, I couldn't let that happen. If Alexa marries anyone, she'll marry me.'

Alexa swallowed at the possessive note in his voice. What would it be like if he truly meant those words? If he actually wanted to marry her for real? And why had that thought even entered her head? She wasn't looking to turn this into a love story. No matter how well he could kiss, Prince Rafaele was completely the wrong kind of man for her.

'This is all very surprising,' King Jaeger said reasonably. 'Why don't we take some time to think about it and agree to meet next week to—?'

'No.' Her father cut the King's offer off before it was fully formed. 'If your brother wants to marry my daughter then the wedding will be held at the end of the month.'

In three weeks!

Her father's words sounded like a death knell in the quiet room. Alexa swallowed hard. This was only meant to be a temporary engagement, not an actual marriage.

'That's not possible,' she choked out. 'I…that is to say, we…'

'This isn't a game, Alexa,' her father interrupted tersely. 'Of his own admission, Prince Rafaele has already experienced cold feet and I will not have another Santarian royal make a fool of you by pulling out at the last minute.' He turned to square off against the Prince. 'If you want my daughter, those are the terms.'

Fully expecting Rafe to run from the room like a man with the devil after him, Alexa wasn't surprised to hear him say, 'The end of the month doesn't work for me. I have a new club opening on that weekend and I have to be there.'

'There you go,' she said, breathing a sigh of relief. 'Now why don't we—?'

'The weekend before then,' her father challenged.

Alexa felt Rafe go dangerously still beside her. Her father didn't move either; his chin jutted out at an angle she knew meant that nothing would get him to back down. They were like two stags facing off against each other over unclaimed territory. Only she was the piece of precious veld they were fighting over.

Deciding she had to do something to defuse the tension in the room, Alexa stepped towards her father, only to have Rafe's hand firm on her hip to hold her in place beside him.

'Tight,' he murmured, his hard gaze flicking from her father's to hers. 'But so be it.'

'So be it? *So be it?*'

Somehow Alexa had convinced her father that she needed a moment alone with her *fiancé*. She moved out of his arms now, and rounded on him.

'Are you completely mad? Why did you say that to him? Why did you agree with his terms?'

'Breathe, Princess,' the Prince ordered curtly, 'before you pass out.'

She wasn't going to pass out. She was going to… Alexa groped for the edge of the sofa behind her and all but fell onto the cushioned seat. She was going to pass out.

'Here.' A glass with amber liquid in it, not unlike the horrible Scotch she'd sipped the night before, was thrust in front of her face. 'Drink this.'

'It's too early for alcohol.'

'It's five o clock somewhere in the world. If you don't drink it, I will.'

'Have it.' Alexa took a deep breath, her palms

against her belly to settle the pitching sensation inside. 'I'm too much in shock to drink it.'

'Why are you so shocked? You're the one who asked me to marry you in the first place.'

'I asked you to cooperate in a fake engagement, not enter into a real marriage.'

'And why *was* that?' His eyes were like blue granite when they met hers. 'You weren't surprised when your father initially disapproved of you marrying me. Was this just an act of rebellion on your part? The perfect, pampered little princess, lashing out against authority by becoming engaged to the Rebel Prince?'

'No!'

Rafe gave a mocking stare. 'Your face gives you away, Princess. Don't ever play poker. You'll lose the bank.'

'Okay, yes, in some small way I was rebelling, but not because I'm perfect, or pampered. Far from it. I don't want to marry anyone right now, and because I knew my father didn't approve of you I never imagined he would push us both to the altar the way that he has.'

'Appears you were wrong.' He paced away from her to stare out of the window. 'It seems the bad brother is just as good for his Princess as the good one.'

Alexa frowned. 'You mean King Jaeger?'

He turned back, his brow lifted in a cynical arch. 'I do only have one brother.'

'I… I've never compared the two of you like that.'

'Like I said, don't play poker.'

'Okay, fine,' Alexa conceded. 'But you can't deny that you're totally different from each other. By your own admission you're not interested in duty and commitment, and you don't care about Santara or politics. Honestly, your life is completely alien to me.'

'Because it's based on pleasure?'

'Because it's hedonistic.' Her face flamed as his eyebrow arched again. 'What I mean is, you do what you want, whenever you want, regardless of what others think of you. You live by your own rules, and I don't know anyone else who does that. Frankly, I envy it.'

For a moment he didn't say anything. Then he sighed and dragged a hand through his overlong hair. Alexa didn't want to remember how thick and soft it had felt beneath her fingertips but she couldn't help it. Her gaze drifted over his unshaven jaw and paused on his well-shaped lips. Lips that were skilled and warm.

Suddenly aware that he was watching her just as closely, she lifted her chin and forced her gaze to remain steady even though she was quaking inside.

'Well, regardless of how this all came about, your father has effectively checkmated us both.'

'So it would seem.' Unable to sit still with so much energy coursing through her body, Alexa rose from the sofa, her mind in a whirl. 'And now we have to un-checkmate ourselves.' Not that she had any idea how to do that. Her father was more stubborn than a mule when he chose to be.

'That won't be possible.'

Alexa frowned as the Prince stared moodily into the glass he was holding.

'It has to be.'

'Not without seriously angering and embarrassing both our Kings.'

Feeling trapped, Alexa absently reached for the glass in his hand, taking a fortifying gulp before handing it back with a grimace. 'So what do we do now?'

'We do what your father wants. We marry. You get to appease your father and help your country and, if you're right, the violence between our countries ceases. I get to pay off a long-standing debt I owe to my brother and ease his load.' He tossed back the remaining contents of the glass and placed it on a low table. 'But nothing else changes. You live in Berenia. I live in London. At a time that is convenient to us both we'll agree that the marriage isn't working and end it.' His gaze sharpened. 'Six months should be long enough.'

'I don't know if that will work. My people will expect you to move to Berenia.'

'I expect billion-dollar deals to fall into my lap every day but unfortunately that doesn't happen either.'

Ignoring his sarcasm, Alexa paced away from him. 'You really think this will work?'

'Why not? I have stories written about me that aren't true all the time. Only this time I'll be the one in charge of creating the story. I find I quite like the idea.'

Alexa gnawed on the inside of her lip in consternation. 'I still think we can find a way out of this if we try.'

'Fine. If you find one, you let me know. As long as it doesn't make things worse for my brother I'll be all over it.'

'And what if six months isn't long enough to convince everyone that this is real?'

'Six months will be plenty. But if you're worried you can just gaze at me adoringly from time to time.'

'That would only feed your ego.'

'Something I'm all for.' His gaze settled on her lips, and heat spiked deep inside her. Suddenly she was thinking about kissing him again and, as if he knew exactly where her mind had gone, his gaze lifted to hers, amusement highlighting the dark blue depths.

Embarrassed, and not a little disconcerted by the strength of her reaction to him, Alexa lifted her chin. 'It will be expected that we're seen together at some point, you know.'

'Perhaps.' His eyes were a hot and watchful brand as they locked with hers. 'But let's cross that bridge when we come to it, hmm?'

If Alexa had wondered over the course of the last two weeks how Prince Rafaele felt about their impending nuptials, all doubt evaporated when she caught sight of his grim expression at the end of the aisle.

He hated it.

Something Alexa would probably have been more aware of had they not delegated every aspect of the wedding planning to their respective assistants.

Not that she'd wanted to plan it. The thought of it had been so challenging she'd deliberately thrown herself into horrendously long working days so that she'd be too exhausted by the end of the day to think about anything at all, least of all the wedding.

The down side to having been so busy was that the time had seemed to rush by. And now she was about to trust her future to a man who liked to be in charge, and whom she hardly knew.

One she was incredibly attracted to.

The unwanted thought entered her head entirely without her permission. For two weeks she'd been trying to avoid thinking about the way he had kissed her and touched her and the way she had responded, but she hadn't been completely successful, her dreams often so erotic she had woken sweaty and embarrassingly aroused on more than one occasion.

Because sex with Prince Rafaele would be unforgettable.

And thinking that way would lead to trouble. They had struck a marriage bargain with each other for political purposes. It was nothing more than a marriage of convenience; the Prince might kiss like a dream but she couldn't have sex with him. Not only would it not serve any long-term purpose but she was very afraid that she'd like it too much. That she'd like *him* too much. And if he were to find her lacking… If he were to find her inadequate… A horrible queasiness settled in the pit of her stomach before she swallowed it down.

No. As tempting as the Prince was the key to making their temporary marriage work was to focus on her objectives—freedom to make her own marriage match in the future, as well as the restoration of political peace between their nations. The latter of which already seemed to be working.

The people of both Berenia and Santara had greeted the announcement of her impending marriage to the Prince with unmistakable enthusiasm, treating it as the love story of the age. That was thanks, mainly, to a photo that had been taken of the two of them dancing at the charity ball. In the photo the Prince was holding her far too close, the smile on his face shockingly sexual, while her own expression was one of stunned stupefaction. At least that was how it looked to her!

But their respective PR departments had loved the photo, adding it to their marriage announcement for the entire world to see.

Alexa eased out a steadying breath as she came to a halt in front of the Prince, her long white gown settling around her ankles in a rustle of silk. If ever there had been a stony-faced groom, he was it.

She swallowed the lump in her throat. If she'd been hoping for some other reaction from him, and maybe deep down she could admit that she had been, then she would have to get over it.

Gone was the devil-may-care seducer she had met at the Santarian Summer Palace just over two weeks ago. Gone was the charming rebel who didn't let anything bother him. This version of the Prince couldn't be more bothered if he was being swarmed by angry wasps, his face carved in stone, his muscles taut as if he were fighting the urge to run.

Join the club, she thought as the celebrant spoke the first words of the service.

As if in a dream state, Alexa barely followed the proceedings, her senses leaping with surprise when the Prince placed his hands on her shoulders and turned her towards him, his fingers sure and strong, his expression unreadable.

Before Alexa fully understood that they had reached the end of the service his head bent to hers, his lips covering her own in a searing kiss. She didn't mean to close her eyes at the contact but she did, and it only heightened the riot of sensations inside of her.

A tremor went through her as his fingertips brushed the nape of her neck in a feather-light caress and Alexa swayed, barely catching herself at the last moment before she completely melted against him.

Fortunately she was able to recover herself as the wedding guests clapped and whooped, and the *qanun* and *oud* struck up a lively tune as they proceeded back down the aisle.

Everyone seemed happy as they ate and danced and mingled during the lavish reception. Everyone except Alexa, who grew more and more miserable as the afternoon wore on. Prince Rafaele had behaved like a polite stranger during most of proceedings and Alexa couldn't wait for him to return to London.

Guilt and nerves ate away at her. Guilt that she had somehow caused this whole debacle with her wretched plan to find a temporary fiancé, and nerves because she had a strange premonition that her life would be changed for ever by marrying him.

Which, of course, it would be—but only temporarily.

And what was the shortest marriage on record? If it was two hours she'd surely beat it because she'd like nothing more than to pretend it hadn't happened at all and end it now.

Badly needing a distraction, she caught sight of King Jaeger, now dancing with his heavily pregnant wife, Queen Regan. Alexa had tried not to like the Queen when she'd first met her, but Regan's compassion and understanding of how she had felt to be jilted by the King had shone through from the start. It was embarrassing now how Alexa had become tearful when she'd first met the Queen, having had to sit through a dinner watching the man she'd had a teenage crush on stare at a woman he clearly adored.

It was strange watching them now because

none of those old feelings she'd had for him seemed to exist any more. She could appreciate his good looks and strong masculine presence but she could no longer see herself by his side. As his wife. Instead she found herself comparing him to her new husband. They both had dark hair and similar eyes and they were both incredibly well built but, as suitable as the King had been as a marriage prospect, he had never drawn her gaze the way Prince Rafaele did.

Alerted by a tingling sensation along the back of her neck, Alexa's eyes cut across the room to find her new husband watching her closely, his face devoid of emotion. She couldn't hold the intensity of his gaze, her face flushed as she found herself admiring the cut of his suit that moulded perfectly to his wide shoulders and lean physique.

It was embarrassing how attractive she found him and the only saving grace was that he'd be returning to London some time in the evening. She couldn't wait for that to happen.

As if reading her desperation for distraction, the King of Santara and his wife approached her.

'May I have this dance, Princess Alexa?'

Alexa swallowed hard as she gazed at the man she had once thought she would marry. While the awareness of what might have been between them was gone, she was still embarrassed by how easily he had cast her aside.

'Please,' Regan encouraged when Alexa automatically turned to her for permission. 'The wedding was beautiful and I hope we can one day become friends as well as sisters-in-law.'

They were sisters-in-law *for now,* but not for ever. She was sure the Queen knew, because Rafaele had told her that he intended to explain the situation to his brother so that he could prepare for when their marriage ended. Alexa had only told Nasrin that their marriage was a sham, not wanting her father to know in case he tried to interfere with her decision.

Ignoring the curiosity of nearby guests as they took to the dance floor together, Alexa pinned what she hoped was a convincing smile to her lips.

'I hope you're having a good time,' King Jaeger murmured as they fell into an easy waltz.

'I am, thank you,' Alexa returned, keeping her misgivings about the wedding to herself. 'I only hope this isn't all for nothing at the end of the day.'

'I have a feeling it won't be,' the King responded enigmatically. 'Although I must confess my surprise in finding my rogue brother in the position of being forced down the aisle so neatly.'

'But you know how that came about,' Alexa said, her voice slightly husky as she gazed into blue eyes that were almost the exact shade as Rafe's, but which didn't make her breath catch at all when she looked into them. 'My father demanded it.'

'True,' he mused softly, a knowing glint in his eyes. 'But not even our father could force Rafa to do something he didn't want to do if he *really* didn't want to do it.'

'Then he met his match in my father,' she said dryly.

'I wonder…' The King smiled. 'My brother is not his usual easy-going self today, and he didn't seem to try all that hard to get out of the wedding.'

As far as Alexa was concerned Rafe had definitely tried to get out of their wedding, and as to his lack of ease…well, that was easily explained. The man had been forced to get married. No doubt that would have wiped the smile off any confirmed bachelor's face.

'My dance, I believe.' Rafaele suddenly cut in, his eyes riveted to where her hand held the King's.

'I was just about to tell Alexa how beautiful she looks,' the King said smoothly. 'Don't you think she looks beautiful?'

'Extremely.' Rafe's eyes narrowed on his brother's, his tone anything but convincing. 'But perhaps if you devoted this much attention to your own wife she wouldn't appear so unhappy,' Rafe prompted lazily, his brow arched.

At that moment a joyous giggle rang out from across the room and they all turned to observe Regan, hand protectively over her baby bump, having a great time with a small group of guests.

'Yes, I can see she feels terrible,' the King drawled, his eyes just as mocking as Rafe's.

The tension between the two men, while not aggressive, was palpable, and again Alexa wondered at the state of their relationship. For two brothers who looked so much alike and who were so close in age they didn't seem overly bonded, the way she had been with Sol.

Alexa gave Rafe a curious look as King Jaeger strolled from the dance floor in the direction of his wife. 'What was that all about?'

'What was what all about?' He gave her a too-innocent look.

'You were rude.'

'Maybe I was jealous.'

'You? Jealous?' Alexa nearly snorted at the prospect. 'Have you ever been jealous before?'

'Not so far.'

'I didn't think so.'

'But then I've never married a woman who was once betrothed to my brother and who gazes adoringly at him every chance she gets.

Are you sure nothing ever happened between the two of you?'

The coolness behind his question took Alexa by surprise. 'Of course not.' Her incredulous gaze met hostile blue. 'Your brother is an honourable man.'

'And I'm not?'

Sensing that his emotions were barely leashed beneath the facade of civility, Alexa moistened her lips. 'I didn't say that. But I was unaware that honour was so important to you.'

'It isn't.' The Prince gave her a benign smile that belied the tension emanating from his large frame. 'As you pointed out previously, I have very different priorities to my brother. That aside, I believe it's time for us to leave, dear wife.'

It took a moment for her mind to process his words but then she frowned. 'What do you mean, *us*?'

'Generally it denotes oneself and the person one happens to be speaking with.'

'Don't be smart,' she retorted. As far as she had understood, Rafe would head back to London alone, claiming that they would take a honeymoon later on, when time permitted. 'I'm not leaving with you. That was never part of the plan.'

'Alas no, but then nor was our actual marriage. But one must improvise.'

'I'm not big on improvising. And we agreed to delay our honeymoon so that we didn't have to have one.'

'Once the international press bought into our *love* story, I thought you'd realise that we would have to present a united front. You were the one who first mentioned that our people would want to see us together, if I remember correctly.'

'Yes, but I was projecting into the future. I can't leave with you now. I have people to see next week. Meetings to take.'

'It's not negotiable, Alexa. I'm not leaving here without you.'

The way he said her name sent a frisson of sensation skittering along her nerve-endings, flustering her. 'Why can't you stay here instead?'

The Prince arched a brow. 'Because it might be a bit hard to open my club from here next weekend—considering it's in Chelsea.'

'Oh.' She hadn't thought of that. 'Well, I need more time to think about this.'

'You have an hour.'

Feeling as if her life was spinning out of control again, Alexa tried to hold her ground. 'Maybe I can join you in a few days.'

'Fine. You do that. And while you're at it you can explain the delay to the press *and* your father, who happens to be watching us closely.'

Knowing she was defeated because she did not want to face her father right now, Alexa groaned. 'But I haven't packed.'

'Throw an overnight bag together. Anything else you need can be sent on.'

'How long do you expect me to be gone?'

'Allow for two weeks. That's the usual time allotted to a honeymoon, isn't it?'

'Honeymoon?'

Her startled gaze met his and something sizzled in the air between them, making it hard to breathe. The room seemed somehow oppressively hot and all Alexa could think about was that blisteringly short kiss at the altar. Her heartbeat picked up and she really wished she knew what he was thinking.

'Not a real honeymoon,' he drawled gruffly. 'Unless that's what you want, of course.'

For a moment Alexa nearly said yes, and the shock of that realisation was enough to have her vigorously shaking her head. 'No, no, it's not.' She hated how she sounded like a frightened rabbit, but it was exactly how she felt.

'I didn't think so.' He gave her a tight smile. 'Which is why we'll spend two weeks in my London apartment. I'll meet you at the palace airstrip in…' he checked his watch '…fifty minutes.'

Fifty minutes?

That was nowhere near long enough for her

to work out how she was going to survive two weeks holed up in an apartment with a man who tempted her like no other, but who couldn't be more wrong for her.

CHAPTER FIVE

RAFE GREW MORE and more agitated the longer
he had to wait on the tarmac for his new wife,
his usual cool deserting him. Not that he had to
wonder too hard to figure out why that was. He
was married. A state he'd thought he'd never find
himself in. And okay, it wasn't a real marriage—
but it damn well felt like one, with the ceremony,
the two hundred plus well-wishers and the stunning bride.

His heart had all but leapt into his throat when
he'd first caught sight of Alexa holding on to her
father's arm at the end of the aisle. Covered head
to toe in a lace gown that had outlined every slim
curve, her floor-length veil hiding her face, she
had been a vision in white.

Over the last couple of weeks he'd told himself that he'd imagined how sensually alluring
she was. Exaggerated how potent his response to
her was. Then she'd walked towards him with a
smooth, graceful stride and he'd known that he

hadn't exaggerated any of it. If anything, he had underestimated her appeal.

A shocking realisation for a man who had decided long ago that he would never let himself be trapped into matrimony under any conditions and now found himself desperately attracted to his wife!

A wife he didn't want, but who he would neatly use to repay Jag for the debt he'd incurred when his brother had been forced to leave his studies and return to Santara to become king after their father had died. At the time Rafe knew the ins and outs of the palace like no one else and could have smoothed the way for his brother, but he'd been desperate to leave and make his own mark on the world and Jag had seen that.

He'd told him to leave, to go find himself, and so far he'd never found cause to call on Rafe to help out. Something that was a little galling, because he'd told Jag that should he ever need him he'd be there.

But Jag had never needed him. However, his brother *had* needed a way to repair the relationship between Santara and Berenia and Rafe had seized the opportunity to repay his debt of gratitude by marrying Alexa.

And he didn't regret it. He hated being in debt to anyone more than anything and doing this for his brother—for his country—would ease his conscience whenever his siblings got up in his face about the way he lived his life.

But that's not the only reason you married her, a sly voice reminded him.

It was a voice he'd ignored over the past two weeks, burying himself in his latest business endeavour to the point of exhaustion. Now, though…now it was hard to deny that perhaps he'd also been under the influence of a shocking sexual attraction when he'd decided to marry Alexa that had exceeded anything he'd experienced before. That, and a deep-seated need to keep her from Lord Richton.

And who's going to keep her from you?

Rafe exhaled roughly. Nobody would keep her from him because nobody would need to. He might want her in his bed but that didn't mean he'd follow through on it. Alexa was not a woman a man toyed with. Not only was she the future queen of Berenia, but she was ultimately looking for something long-term, something permanent, and the last thing he wanted was to sleep with her and give her the impression that he was the right man for her.

Because he was most definitely not that man.

A truth that bothered him, though why it should he couldn't fathom. He'd never wanted to be any woman's 'right' man. Ever. His life was just fine as it was, even if Alexa believed it to be 'hedonistic'.

He shook his head. A Buddhist monk probably had a more exciting life than he had of late. Even the Spanish supermodel hadn't inspired him enough to take her to his bed while they'd been dating.

But Alexa did. Alexa, with her potent combination of steel and sweetness. Alexa who he couldn't seem to get out of his head. Who lit a fire inside of him that made his body throb with need.

Alexa who he wasn't going to touch.

And no doubt she'd be happy with that decision if the horrified expression on her face when he'd raised her veil at the altar was anything to go by.

He exhaled a long breath and rechecked his watch. Realistically, he'd only been waiting on her for twenty minutes. It felt like twenty years.

And then finally she appeared from the side door of the palace, looking extremely tantalising in a casual pair of jeans and a lightweight jacket held closed with a zip that begged to be tugged downwards, the cool desert breeze teasing the long strands of her ponytail.

For some reason the tension inside his chest eased at the sight of her. Had he been worried she wouldn't show?

Irritated at the very idea, he scowled down at her. 'I hope you have a thicker jacket than that. March in London isn't exactly warm.'

Jewel-green eyes blinked up at him and he reminded himself that this situation wasn't exactly her fault so he needed to calm down.

'I believe Nasrin packed one, yes.'

Her assistant, who stood behind her, nodded enthusiastically. 'I did, Your Highness. I also know that you stowed your laptop into your satchel before you left.' She gave Alexa a firm look. 'No matter who contacts you, your father specifically told me that you are on your honeymoon and therefore not to do any work.'

Alexa stiffened at the mention of their 'honeymoon' but then gave her assistant a warm smile. 'Duly noted.'

Nasrin made an unconvinced sound in the back of her throat, piquing Rafe's interest in their relationship. Alexa had a reputation for being cool and remote, and yet it was clear that she and this woman shared a strong connection that went beyond simple employee and employer. There weren't many things Rafe admired more than those in positions of power treating the people who served them with respect and kindness.

'Ready to leave?' he asked, aware that as he spoke her body went stiff with tension. Which irritated him even more. How were they going to convince anyone that their union was more than a marriage of convenience if she turned to stone every time he spoke to her?

Forcing his eyes away from her jeans-clad butt as she preceded him up the stairs, Rafe stopped to speak with his pilot while Alexa buckled herself into her seat. No doubt she wouldn't be impressed by his plane. He might be a prince, but he wasn't a king. He couldn't offer her anything that she didn't already have.

And why was he even thinking like this? Their marriage wasn't real. It wasn't even damned convenient when it came down to it. It wasn't anything. They were two people who were doing each other a favour. So why did something that wasn't supposed to be monumental feel as if it was?

The circular nature of his thoughts warred with the constant need to put his hands on her and did little to restore his usual good humour. He wasn't sure anything could.

Using work to distract himself, he opened his laptop to go over the latest specs on a building he'd just purchased in Scotland. It was a grand old edifice that had once been a cinema and his COO was urging him to tear it down rather than restore it because the cost would be exorbitant. There was something charming about it though and, while he was all about the bottom line, he had an inclination to go in the other direction this time.

He wondered what Alexa would make of it and then scowled at the thought. It wasn't as if he was going to ask her. He might have to live with her for the next two weeks but that didn't mean they had to interact. In fact the less they saw of each other the better. Because wanting her was driving him to distraction.

Perhaps he could discreetly settle her into a hotel, then he wouldn't have to see her at all. Which would work right up until the press got hold of the information and blew their whole 'love story' out of the water.

'Sorry.' She gave him a small smile. 'I feel sort of responsible for all of this honeymoon palaver, and I know you're not happy about it.'

'You're not responsible.'

'Well, at least you didn't try to make me feel better by pretending to be happy.' She gave a strained laugh. 'But I know you didn't want anything to change and it clearly has.'

'That was a bit short-sighted, given the monumental interest in our wedding.'

'Yes. It seems that my father was right about our marriage moving everyone's attention from problems to pleasure. Do you know they even have a mug and tea towels with our faces on it?'

'Quaint.' He noticed the purple smudges beneath her eyes that he hadn't seen before and wondered if she'd had as little sleep as he'd had over the past fortnight.

'I know. My people went all-out. I think after your brother ditched me no one thought I'd ever find anyone else to marry.'

At the mention of his brother Rafe was reminded of the way she'd gazed at Jag only hours earlier. It had appalled him to think that she might still have feelings for his brother, and he didn't like it.

'Why would anyone think that you wouldn't get married? You're the heir to the throne of Berenia.'

'Thanks for pointing out my most saleable quality.'

Her self-deprecating tone made him frown. 'That is not your most saleable quality.'

He'd say her lips were definitely high on the list. Along with her legs, and the keen intelligence that shone from those magnificent green eyes. 'My brother fell in love with someone else. That was hardly your fault.'

'Some saw it differently.'

Noting the way her shoulders had tensed, Rafe's eyes narrowed. 'Define "differently".'

'I can barely remember.' She waved her hand between them as if the whole thing was inconsequential. 'Something about me not being womanly enough to keep hold of him.'

Rafe made a rude noise in the back of his throat. 'I've never heard anything more ridiculous.'

Or wrong.

'Anyway.' She made another flicking gesture with her hand. 'I was thinking that if your apartment isn't big enough for the both of us, then I could stay in a hotel.'

Even though Rafe had come up with the same idea only moments earlier, the fact that she would prefer a hotel to his home chafed. 'My apartment is big enough.'

'Still, I could—'

'It's big enough.'

'You didn't let me finish.'

'I didn't have to. How do you think it would look if I set my beautiful wife up in a hotel straight after our wedding?'

'I suppose.' She fidgeted with her phone so he knew there was more coming. 'And your staff? Will they think it strange when we have separate bedrooms?'

Rafe lazily leaned back in his seat, relaxing now that he knew what her angle was. 'Is that your way of telling me that sex is off the table, Alexa?'

As he expected, her eyes flashed and turned

frosty. 'Of course sex is off the table. It was never actually on the table.'

'Really?'

Hot colour poured into her cheeks and he knew she was recalling every hungry kiss they'd shared, just as he was. 'That wasn't the impression I got.'

And no way would he let her paint it any other way.

'I'm sorry you got a different impression,' she said stiffly, refusing to meet his eye, 'but I'm not interested in meaningless sex.'

Meaningless sex?

He regarded her steadily. 'Who said it would be meaningless?'

She shifted in her seat, unwittingly drawing his gaze to her body. He could see the outline of her rounded breasts beneath the fitted jacket and his body clenched as he recalled how perfectly she'd fitted into the palm of his hand.

'What else could it be?' she said, bringing his eyes back to hers. 'And, regardless, it would only blur the lines between us. So there's no reason for us to become intimate.'

Her voice was matter of fact, her reasoning completely logical. So logical that he agreed with it. Unfortunately he didn't care. This thing between them pulled at his self-control and her ready denial of its existence only made him want to prove her wrong.

'I can think of at least one.' In fact right now he had about one hundred and one filtering through his brain. 'Pure, unadulterated pleasure.'

'Oh.' The soft catch in her voice fired his blood. It made him want to reach over and haul her out of her seat and into his.

As if reading him correctly her face flamed. 'I'm not that...*physical*...but, since you obviously are, I don't mind if you seek...*relief* elsewhere. I only ask that you be discreet about it.'

It took Rafe a moment to fully understand what she meant and then he didn't even try to hide his incredulity.

'You're giving me permission to cheat on you? What kind of wife does that?'

'The non-real variety. Obviously.'

'Princess, while I'd love to live up to this wild image you have of me as some sort of sexual deviant, not every relationship I have with a woman ends between the sheets. And, to answer your earlier question, I only have one full-time housekeeper, apart from my security personnel, and she won't ask any questions.'

'Good to know.'

What was good to know? That he didn't sleep with every woman he met, or that his housekeeper wouldn't care about their sleeping arrangements?

His mouth thinned. She was driving him crazy and when she coolly turned her attention to her phone he decided to drive her a little crazy in return. 'Alexa…' He waited for her eyes to reconnect with his before leaning toward her to whisper throatily. 'Sex between us wouldn't be meaningless at all. It would be mind-blowing.'

It was nearly midnight when the plane touched down in London and Rafe ushered Alexa into a waiting limousine.

She had spent most of the flight vacillating between being mortified that she'd told Rafe about the rumours pertaining to her lack of femininity and growing hot at the thought of what mind-blowing sex with him would feel like.

She knew better than to air her dirty laundry in public and what had she wanted him to say? That she *was* womanly enough to hold a man?

Wishing she could just curl up and sleep for the next two weeks, Alexa did her best to ignore the man beside her and take in what she could see of the city.

She'd been in London once before for a state dinner but she'd had no time to explore at all, flying in and out within twenty-four hours, due to work commitments.

It must have rained before they arrived because the streets were shiny and black, the twinkling lights outlining a world that was miles away from what she was used to.

In no time at all, it seemed, the big Mercedes pulled into the underground car park of an impressive plate glass ten-storey building.

Yawning, Alexa barely noticed the high-tech layout of the garage, or the impressive array of luxury cars parked in personalised bays.

She did, however, notice the state-of-the-art glass-encased lift that whisked them to the top floor and opened out into a polished marble foyer lined with a dark wood finish.

'The building is patrolled by Chase Security,' Rafe informed her, 'a high-level security firm, and all the windows are bulletproof. Two of your secret service detail will be arriving later on tonight. I've organised for them to have a lower level apartment while you're here. A concierge is on duty twenty-four-seven if you should need anything and I'm not here.'

He walked through to a living area with twelve-foot ceilings and enormous windows on three sides that gave an incredible view over the park and the city beyond. An ultra-modern monochrome chandelier hung from the high ceiling, perfectly setting off the sectional furniture that was both homely and state-of-the-art.

Even though she lived in a palace, the architectural elegance of Rafe's home took her breath away. 'It's beautiful,' she said reverently. 'Like a castle in the clouds.'

Glancing up from checking mail that had been neatly placed on a display table, Rafe gave her a mocking glance. 'The ceiling chains are in the bedroom.'

'Ceiling chains?'

'It's par for the course with being a *hedonist*. Isn't that the word you used?'

Alexa groaned as he threw that back in her face, but really, what did he expect her to think when he made so little effort to refute any of the wicked claims made about him? In fact, he'd basically told her they were all true!

'Are you saying I've got it wrong?'

His mouth twisted into a cynical line. 'I'm saying I had a good time in my twenties. Make of that what you will.'

Alexa thought about everything she'd read about him, and everything she knew to date. So far he didn't seem all that self-absorbed at all, and he *had* stopped kissing her in the library when she'd asked him to. In fact, he'd given her fair warning that he was going to do so, thereby giving her enough time to say no. Not that he'd given her fair warning the second time. The second time he'd taken her in his arms on the terrace she'd all but swooned at his feet.

'Here's the thing, Alexa.' His voice sounded all soft and growly. 'I like sex, but I like straight up bedroom sex. Sometimes I like shower sex or spa sex. I've even been known to enjoy table sex and floor sex. I leave kinky sex for those who enjoy it more.'

Knowing he was trying to shock her with his litany of sexual venues, Alexa ignored the jolt of pleasure from just hearing him say the word. 'Does that mean that the whips are in the bedroom too?'

Clearly surprised by her comeback, his mouth twitched. 'No.' Heading for the doorway, he gestured for her to follow him. 'I keep those in the safe.'

She couldn't help laughing, and it relieved some of the tension that had plagued her since she'd walked down the aisle towards him.

'I've asked Mrs Harrington to prepare one of the guest suites for your use down this hallway. If you want to use the pool or gymnasium they're on the lower level and the library is on the mezzanine above to your right.'

'I thought apartments were small,' Alexa said, admiring the artwork on the walls as she passed. 'You like the Impressionists?'

'I like all art as long as it's not a landscape. I prefer the real thing to a painting.'

'I feel the same.'

Alexa couldn't hold back a smile as she took in the gorgeous honey-toned bedroom with a view of glowing city lights that spread for miles. Her eyes darted to the ceiling with impish humour, but she wished she hadn't because now he was looking at her lips and she couldn't breathe properly.

Sexual awareness pulled at her insides, worse than it had done all day, and the quiet of the apartment highlighted that for once it was just the two of them. Alone. Together.

As if feeling the same pull she did, Rafe stepped back. 'Your private bathroom is through the walk-in closet. Stevens will be up with your bags in a moment.'

Trying to steady her breathing so he didn't see how badly he affected her, Alexa dropped her handbag onto the king-sized bed that faced the wall of windows. 'I probably won't sleep tonight anyway. This view is incredible.'

'That's up to you. I intend to sleep very well. Goodnight, Alexa.'

Watching him leave through the reflection in the windows, Alexa let out a slow breath. She couldn't deny the effect Rafe had on her. Especially after he'd listed off places where he liked to have sex.

Good lord!

But being intimate with a man like the rebel Prince of Santara would be like driving a Formula One racing car on a suburban road.

Deadly at every turn, but, oh, so much fun.

And why was she even countenancing such a thought when she'd already made her position on intimacy clear? But she knew why, didn't she? She was attracted to him. Incredibly attracted and no logical reasoning or denial made a difference to how she felt.

And it was something she needed to work on. Because even knowing that he was the most unsuitable man on the planet, and that there was no chance she would ever imagine herself in love with him, she couldn't deny that just looking at him made her body crave something she had no experience to deal with.

At least not objectively. And she could not afford to fall into her old ways and get *emotional* over him. Because he certainly wouldn't get emotional over her. No one ever had and it hurt, knowing that men found it so easy to walk away from her.

And Prince Rafaele would definitely walk away from her; it was what he did with all women. It was why she had married him in the first place. She wanted him to walk away from her in the end.

Restless, she moved to stand in front of the tall windows, trying to figure out why she felt so unsettled.

Was it just the pomp and ceremony of the day? Was it exhaustion from lack of sleep? Or was it that tonight was her wedding night and she was spending it alone? Alone, overlooking a picturesque night sky in a beautiful room with a bed the size of a swimming pool, and an ache deep inside her that longed to be satisfied. An ache to have Rafe touch her again, kiss her again...

'Your Highness?'

A voice outside her door broke into thoughts that were rapidly spiralling out of control. Ushering the chauffeur into her room, she thanked him for delivering her luggage and immediately set out to find her nightwear. All she needed was a good night's sleep. She only hoped it didn't elude her yet again...

Fortunately it didn't and she woke feeling more refreshed than she had anticipated. After a quick shower she donned her yoga gear, stretched on her yoga mat until she felt all the kinks leave her body, then went in search of coffee.

Following one hallway to the next, she eventually found the kitchen, a beautiful room of shiny stainless steel and polished wood. The state-of-the-art coffee machine took almost as long to locate. It was set into the wall above the oven, and the various buttons and dials looked like they belonged on a flight panel rather than on a coffee machine. Having only ever fixed herself a coffee from a small machine in her private suite, Alexa had no idea how it worked.

Still, how difficult could it be to operate? She opened a few cupboards until she located a mug and set it under the central cylinder that looked like it dispensed coffee.

Gnawing on the inside of her lip, she hoped that if she started pressing buttons she wouldn't blow the thing up.

Before she could decide which one to push, however, she felt Rafe's presence behind her.

'What are you doing?'

Alexa glanced over her shoulder to see her husband standing in the doorway. He was dressed for business in a pale blue fitted shirt buttoned all the way to the wide column of his tanned throat, and a royal blue silk tie that turned his eyes the same shade.

Beautiful. He was utterly beautiful and Alexa did her best to calm the spike in her heart rate.

'I'm studying your coffee machine and trying

to figure out how not to break it,' she said, giving a tentative smile.

Probably the best thing going forward would be for them to become friends. Anything would be better than the sense of awkwardness she currently felt. 'You don't have an instruction manual, do you?'

His eyes narrowed even more as his gaze swept over her with cool indifference. 'What type of coffee do you want?'

'A soy latte. If it does that.'

'This thing could probably reboot NASA,' he growled, coming up behind her and reaching over her shoulder, stabbing his finger at the buttons. 'Let me show you how it works.'

He started going through the various options and Alexa tried to concentrate but his heat and clean woodsy scent were doing crazy things to her brain. The urge to turn her face into the crook of his neck and sniff it was incredibly powerful and it took every lesson she'd ever learned in how to be objective to prevent herself from actually doing so.

By the time she'd mastered the urge the lesson was over.

'Then you hit Start.'

Great, she hadn't learned a thing.

Moments later the machine hissed and gurgled and Rafe handed her a perfectly made coffee.

Breathing the aroma deep into her lungs, Alexa groaned gratefully, her sexual awareness of the man in front of her immediately superseded by the need for caffeine. Which lasted right up until she opened her eyes and saw his dark gaze fixed on her mouth. Heat and desire swept through her at a blinding rush but, as if he hadn't felt a thing in return, he stepped back from her and fetched an espresso cup from an overhead cupboard.

Seriously disturbed by how easily he made her want him, Alexa racked her brain for something to say that would ease the tension between them.

'So you're off to work then,' she said, silently cringing at the obvious statement.

'It pays the bills.'

'And do you work at your nightclubs or an office?'

'Both.'

Okay, then. So he wasn't going to make this easy.

Unperturbed, Alexa leant against a glossy cabinet, watching him reset the machine. 'You know I'd really love to come to the opening of your club this Friday night. I've never been to a nightclub before.'

'No.'

Alexa blinked with surprise at his curt tone. 'No?'

'That's what I said.'

'Why not?'

'You're too straight.'

'Too straight?' She scowled at him. 'What does that mean?'

'It means what it means,' he dismissed in a way that only ratcheted up her annoyance. 'And I have no intention of arguing with you about it. It's too early in the morning, for a start.'

'Then don't be obnoxious.'

'I'm not being obnoxious.' His brows drew down, matching the set of his mouth. 'You're not the clubbing type. If you want to do touristy things like shopping or going to the West End or the ballet, just let me know and I'll have Hannah arrange it.'

'Hannah?' She was completely miffed at his condescension. 'One of your old girlfriends?'

'She's my assistant.'

Oh, right. She remembered Nasrin mentioning Hannah now that she thought about it, but she'd been too incensed by his attitude to place her. 'I'm nowhere near as straight as you seem think I am,' she said, wondering what he would say if she told him about how she had gone behind her father's back to be with Stefano.

'Yes, you are.'

He retrieved his coffee and turned to face the kitchen windows as if that was the end of the discussion.

Infuriated, Alexa glared at his wide back. 'You're as immovable as my father,' she snapped, her temper spiking. 'And you think you know everything, just as he does.'

'Alexa—'

'Are you usually this grouchy or is it having me here in your space that's making you so unreasonable?'

'I'm not a morning person.'

'You don't say. Well, I am, and when you walked in before I thought maybe we could find some common ground between us, maybe even become friends, to make the next two weeks easier, but you're really making me rethink that strategy.'

Rafe let out a rough breath as if the very sight of her annoyed him. 'Good. It's best if we're not friends.'

Not having expected such a brutal response, Alexa blinked. 'Then what would you suggest?'

He paused, his blue eyes as stormy as the Atlantic as he stared at her. 'Nothing. I suggest nothing.'

Alexa's brows shot up. 'So you want me to come up with all the ideas?'

'No.' He pushed a lock of hair back from his forehead, clearly frustrated. 'I meant that we literally do nothing. This isn't a forever thing, Alexa. We're here because I mucked up and let chemistry get in the way of rational thinking. That won't happen again.'

'By chemistry you mean——'

'Sexual attraction. Biology.' His eyes pinned her to the spot and all she could think about was sex. Something hot and dark passed between them before he blinked, deliberately severing the connection. 'I'm referring to this thing between us that you'd like to pretend doesn't exist. Fortunately, it will fade soon enough. In the meantime I don't need to know if you're a morning person or a night person and I don't want to know if there is any common ground between us. If you want this to go easier you'll stay on your side of the bed—metaphorically speaking—and I'll stay on mine.'

Shaken by the harshness of his tone, and her own hurt response at how little he wanted to do with her, Alexa hid her emotions behind an arched brow. 'Okay, well, that does make it easier. Now I don't have to rack my brain trying to make small talk while I'm here. Thanks for the heads-up.'

'Alexa——'

'You know, if you ever get sick of women falling in love with you, just show them your grouchy side. It will cure them of any fantasies straight away.' She kept her tone deliberately light but she could tell by his frown that he wasn't buying it. Still, she didn't care. She was close to tears because, after their brief moment of camaraderie the night before, she'd thought he liked her, if only a little.

But that was what came from being too needy and she'd thought she'd learned that lesson a long time ago.

And suddenly she was assailed by a feeling of loneliness she hadn't felt since Sol had died, old feelings of inadequacy threatening to swamp her.

'Alexa—'

'Sorry, I have to go.' Knowing that her emotions were way too close to the surface and refusing to cry in front of another man who didn't want her, she quickly dumped the cold remains of her coffee in the sink and rinsed the mug. 'I'm all sweaty after my yoga workout. Thanks for the coffee. Have a nice day.'

Escaping down the hall, she headed for her bedroom, her ears straining to hear if he followed her. Of course he hadn't. Why would he?

She released a breath she told herself was relief, an ache in her chest she didn't want to acknowledge. What did she care if he didn't want to be friends? She didn't need his friendship either. She didn't need anything from him.

Grabbing her laptop from her satchel, she set it on the bed and typed in her passcode. Two weeks stretched before her as endless as two years, and

she pulled up the files she'd been working on before the wedding.

If she did nothing else, these two weeks she
could at least work. There was plenty of it, and
she had to prove to her father that she could do
this. And to herself. Besides, anything was better than this horrible hollow feeling of rejection
inside her chest that she had never wanted to
feel again.

CHAPTER SIX

A MAN'S HOME was usually his castle, but right now Rafe's castle—his 'castle in the clouds'—felt more like a prison. Only it wasn't a prison keeping him locked in; it was a prison keeping him locked out. This past week he'd found it safer staying at the office for as long as possible rather than risk returning home, where he might run into his delectable wife.

But even for a man who kept long hours, this routine was exhausting, especially since it was past midnight for the fourth night this week and he still wasn't home.

It was either stay away or be rude to Alexa again, as he had been that first morning. Finding her in tight-fitting yoga gear, frowning at his coffee machine like a cute disgruntled kitten, had nearly had him lifting her onto the counter, stepping between her legs and telling her that the only instruction she needed was in how to pleasure him.

Just thinking about it was enough to make

his body burn. So instead he'd been rude and hurt her when he'd dismissed her invitation of friendship. And he hadn't liked hurting her. Hadn't liked dimming the light in her clear, green eyes.

Normally he was laid-back and calm. Normally he'd come home from a hard day at work and put on some rock music, maybe play a little jazz or classical Chopin depending on his mood. Sometimes he'd grab a cold beer from the fridge and turn on the football, catch up on some of the highlights. Other times, if he was tired after a night networking at one of his clubs, or being with a woman, he'd grab whatever Mrs Harrington had left for him in the fridge, wash it down with an accompanying Burgundy and head straight to bed.

Simple. Easy.

He rarely questioned his routine, and if he ever felt a little lonely, or restless, he hit the gym.

Now he found himself looking for signs of Alexa in his home. Like the sweater she'd left over the back of a chair last night, and the hairband she'd left in the kitchen the night before that. He probably owed her an apology for being so distant all week, but that would involve speaking to her and the last thing he wanted to do was to encourage her to want to be 'friends' again. Friends didn't want to tear the other person's clothes off at just the sight of them, so that was out of the question.

'We're here, sir,' Stevens said, alerting him to the fact that he was sitting in the back of the Mercedes and the engine wasn't even running.

'Great.'

He gave Stevens a curt nod and headed for his lift, thankful when he found his apartment shrouded in darkness because it meant that Alexa would be once again in bed.

Placing his computer bag on the sofa, he noticed a pair of socks sitting on the side table, along with an empty mug of herbal tea and a scattering of magazines.

Shaking his head, he wondered how he was supposed to forget she was living with him when she left tiny reminders of her presence lying around. Not to mention the sweet scent of her perfume that lingered in the air.

Gritting his teeth, he dumped her mug in the sink and her socks in the laundry before heading to his room.

Strangely, keeping people at a distance and compartmentalising his life had never been one of his issues before, but he had to admit that he was struggling with Alexa.

Nine days.

That was all he had left of her stay in his home.

If he survived it with his sanity intact he'd deserve more than a gold star.

He'd deserve her.

Biting back an oath at the ridiculousness of that thought, he decided to ignore his hollow stomach and head for bed. God knew he didn't want to tempt fate and run into the woman in his kitchen again. Which was when he noticed a light glowing from beneath his library door.

Hoping Alexa had left the light on by mistake and wouldn't be inside, he was pulled up short when he opened the door to find her slumped over the antique desk in the corner.

With his heart in his mouth, he strode towards her, hoping with every breath in his body that there was nothing wrong with her.

'Alexa?'

He reached out and gently shook her shoulder, relieved beyond reason when she made a small snuffling sound and buried her face against her arm.

Thank God. She wasn't unconscious, or worse, and his heart rate steadied once more.

She looked angelic in sleep, her glorious hair piled on top of her head in a messy topknot. Rejecting his body's immediate reaction to the sight of her, he frowned as he took in the mountain of paperwork scattered over the desk.

Work, he realised as he studied the papers,

remembering how her assistant had told her she wasn't to do any. She must have printed the documents from the laptop that was on sleep mode beside her.

'Alexa?' He tried again to rouse her but she gave another grumpy little whimper and tried to flick him away. Presumably, since she was a morning person, she wouldn't be chirpy at being woken in the middle of the night.

He found he quite liked seeing her all rumpled and sleepy, and then cut the thought off at the knees.

'Alexa, you need to wake up.'

Coming to with a start, she blinked up at him, and it was all Rafe could do not to reach down and kiss the sleepy pout from her lips. To distract himself he jerked his glance in the direction of the papers spread around her. 'Have you been at this all day?'

'Oh, hello.' She yawned and stretched her arms above her head. 'Mostly. It took longer than I thought. I did go for a walk in Hyde Park, but I had to put the sightseeing I planned on hold— Oh, sorry, I didn't mean to bore you.' She glanced away from him and when she spoke next her tone was decidedly frosty, as if she'd recalled their last interaction and hated him. 'What time is it? No, don't answer that. I'll find out for myself.'

'It's after midnight. And you don't have to treat me like a villain.'

'I'm not,' she said coolly, stacking her papers together.

Rafe scowled. 'Have you been at this all night? You'll wear yourself out if this is the pace you keep in Berenia.'

'That's not your concern.'

'Okay.' He held his hands up in front of him. 'Will it help if I apologise for being a first-rate jerk the other morning?'

She glanced up at him from beneath long sooty lashes, and Rafe's jaw clenched against the punch of instant attraction.

'Perhaps.'

'Then I'm sorry. I wasn't in a great mood, but I don't want you to feel uncomfortable around me.'

'I don't. I've had work to do.'

Which brought him back to how tired she looked. 'Work you're not supposed to be doing.'

She shrugged. 'Someone has to do it or it won't get done.'

'Delegate.'

'It's not that simple. We need to hire new staff, and—'

'Duty called.'

'Yes. Something I would have thought you would understand even if you don't like it.'

'I understand it. I even lived it for a time, particularly when Jag was studying in the US. Unfortunately, I didn't live up to my father's expectations as a suitable fill-in.'

She blinked at his harsh tone. 'How could you not?'

Rafe's jaw hardened. 'I wasn't Jag.'

A slight frown marred her forehead, her eyes fixed on his as if she saw more than he had intended her to see. 'But that's—'

'Irrelevant.' He cut off her sympathetic response. He never talked about the past. Not even with his siblings. 'If the people of Santara should ever need me I would be there for them, but this isn't about me. This is about you needing to find balance.' He perched on the edge of the desk, his fingers itching to push back the strand of hair that curved over her cheek. 'I told you before that you need to say no more often.'

'I'm not good at no.' She gave him a brief look. 'I suppose that makes me the dutiful little mouse in your eyes but—'

'I should never have said that,' Rafe interjected. 'You're dedicated and focused and that will make you a great queen, but you should stand up for yourself more.'

'Well, thanks. For the compliment.' She huffed out a breath. 'As to the rest... I do try to say no, but there's so much to learn. And it's so easy to make a mistake.'

'Mistakes are *how* we learn.'

'They're not how *I* want to learn.' She shook her head. 'They cost too much.'

Rafe frowned at the vehemence in her voice. 'You're speaking from experience.' And not a good one, he guessed.

'Yes, but we all make mistakes, don't we?' she replied defensively. 'Even you.'

'I don't deny it. Most of mine get splashed across the Internet. But I doubt you've ever made a mistake worth talking about.'

She narrowed her eyes and took the bait as he hoped she would. 'I told you the other morning that I'm not as straight as you think I am. I nearly caused a scandal once.'

Rafe raised an eyebrow. 'I doubt that.'

'You think me so boring?'

'I don't think you're boring at all.' He thought she was the most beguiling woman he'd ever met and, to his surprise, he wanted to know her secrets. Especially this one. 'Tell me about your scandal.'

Her lips twisted distastefully and for a moment he thought she'd tell him to mind his own business again.

'I was seventeen and naive.' She arched a brow

as if daring him to mock her. 'He was Italian with nice arms and he worked in the stables.'

'Ah, I think I see where this is going,' he said, hoping he was wrong. 'Pray, continue.'

'It's not that ground-breaking, actually… He told me that he loved me and took me to bed. Then he went straight to my father and used my virginity as a bargaining chip so we'd be forced to get married.'

She was right; the story wasn't ground-breaking, just totally humiliating for the one who had been used so callously.

Knowing how bad it felt to be judged out of hand, he kept his tone as light as hers. 'I take it that your father didn't exactly jump for joy at the information and welcome him into the household with open arms.'

Alexa gave him a wry grin. 'I still don't know how much he paid Stefano to leave and never contact me again, but sometimes, when I'm feeling particularly low, I like to imagine that he put the country into debt because of it.'

Rafe laughed at her dryness, but it didn't stop him from wanting to shove this Stefano's teeth down his throat and bury him beneath the blazing sun with just his head showing, as his ancestors would have done.

'If you give me his full name I could find him

and have the Chase brothers beat the cretin to a pulp.'

Unless he got to him first, of course.

'You'd do that for me?' She blinked at him in surprise, as if no one had suggested it before. 'Not even my father said that, and you're the ultimate heartbreaker. You leave women crying all the time.'

'That is not true,' he said curtly, for the first time wishing that his playboy reputation didn't exist. 'I only enter relationships with women who know that I won't fall in love with them, and I'm upfront and honest about that from the beginning. If they cry when it ends it's not because I duped them.'

Her green eyes grew thoughtful. 'How do you know you won't fall in love with them?'

'Because I don't need love. And I make sure to never confuse emotion with sex.'

She paused as if that information required some effort to digest. 'I need to be more like that. But at least Stefano taught me what to look out for when it comes to choosing a life partner. Or what *not* to look out for.'

'What he should have taught you was how good it can be between a man and a woman in bed.'

He saw her throat constrict at his words and suddenly his hands itched to touch her. That Italian idiot might not have been able to show her a good time, but now Rafe couldn't stop thinking about how much he wanted to replace her bad memories with good ones that he'd personally created.

Needing to stop himself from reaching for her and doing something he'd later regret, he pushed away from the desk.

'We should go to bed.'

Alexa blinked at him, her eyes as wide as a baby owl's. 'Together?'

The muscle in his jaw clenched tight as his brain easily conjured up an image of her naked on his sheets. Before he could figure out how to respond to that, a streak of hot, mortified colour scored along her cheekbones. 'Forget I said that. I'm clearly more tired than I thought.'

Wanting to defuse the situation, Rafe nodded. 'I get it. My club is opening tomorrow night and I could use a few hours myself.'

'Right.' She blinked up at him from beneath long silky lashes. 'About that. Am I still banned from your club?'

'Yes.' No way did he want her at one of his clubs, distracting him constantly.

'Won't that look strange?' she persisted. 'As your wife I would be expected to go to support you.'

'I don't need support.'

'Everyone needs support. But, regardless, the media will expect to see me there. I take it you are having a media presence.'

'Only for a couple of hours. No one will know you're not there.'

She mulled that over and then tilted her chin up at a belligerent angle.

'I'd like to go.'

Not wanting to get into a debate with her when his brain and body were mutually stuck on images of her naked and wanting, Rafe sighed. 'Alexa—'

'You've just told me I should stand up for myself more. Not to take no for an answer.'

'I believe I said you should start saying no more often.'

'Something you're really good at. But it amounts to the same thing. Taking charge of my needs. And I'd like to see your club. So I'm taking charge.'

Rafe ran a hand through his hair, a frustrated growl leaving his throat. 'I didn't mean for you to start "taking charge" with me.'

Her sudden smile made his heart kick against his ribs.

'For some reason I feel safe with you.'

'The last thing I am is safe.' Especially with the visions currently going through his head. When she didn't respond, or back down as he'd hoped, he shook his head. 'Fine. I'll arrange a car to pick you up at ten.'

'Ten? Isn't that a bit late?'

'That's early by London standards. Nothing happens before then.'

'Ten. Okay, got it.' Her eyes sparkled like clean-cut emeralds, her happiness making his heartbeat quicken.

'If you need anything before then, or change your mind, I'll have Hannah on standby to help out.'

'I won't change my mind. And you won't regret this.' She was almost vibrating with excitement. 'You won't even know I'm there. Promise.'

Rafe groaned silently at the enormous smile on her face. He should have left her asleep at the desk.

Pacing the upper floor office suite at Bound, Rafe watched on a bank of security monitors as guests continued to pour through the front door of the club, each one wide-eyed with delight as they took in the chrome and glass chandeliers and the Dalí-inspired decor.

'So far, so good,' Hannah, his assistant, ventured beside him. A pocket rocket, Hannah had the energy of a racehorse, which was probably why she hadn't quit on him like so many of his other EAs had done over the years.

Rafe grunted in acknowledgement. At this point he didn't much care about the success of the club. He just wanted to know where Alexa was.

'Oh, relax,' Hannah admonished as she saw him check his watch again. 'I organised Chase Security to travel in with her as well as her own security detail, as you instructed. Between the lot of them, you'd think she was bringing the heads of state of fifty nations with her. But she should be here any minute.'

'Since when do I worry?' Rafe said, not bothering to hide his irritation.

Hannah's grin widened before she checked a message that popped up on her tablet. 'Since you got married, it seems. But I can see why you married her. We had a great time shopping. She's truly lovely. Not at all stuck-up, as one might expect from royalty, but then you're not stuck up, so I don't know why I thought she would be. And she looks incredible in her new dress. We had a lot of fun choosing it. Oh, I better go. The Duke and Duchess of Crenshore have arrived and I need to show them to their private table.'

Not hearing a word she'd said after 'new dress', Rafe's mind was now obsessed with exactly what this new dress would look like. Would her hair be up or down? He still had no idea how long it was. Another unwanted obsession he'd suddenly developed.

Glancing once more at the display showing the entrance, Rafe saw one of the Chase Security guards he'd organised to shadow Alexa walk through the door.

Not realising he was holding his breath, he waited for Alexa to appear and exhaled at seeing her.

Her hair was down. And it was long. Almost waist-length and as straight as an arrow.

Wearing a trench coat and stiletto heels, she looked regal and calm except for the glitter in her eyes that gave away her excitement as she scanned the foyer.

A similar feeling went through him now and he did his best to douse it. There was no reason he should be 'excited' that she was here. He'd agreed to let her come because he felt sorry for her, stuck in his apartment working. She worked too much, trying to prove herself, as he had once done. Only she was perfect as she was.

Stopping those thoughts dead in their tracks, he noted with satisfaction how her security detail scanned the crowd before allowing her to move further inside. It was guests only at the club tonight, and Rafe had personally checked over the list and given it to her team to cross-reference, but he didn't want to take any chances with her safety.

For some reason I feel safe with you.

A muscle ticked in his jaw. She'd been talking about taking charge of her professional needs, but his mind was still stuck on her 'taking charge' in a much more pleasurable capacity.

Cursing at the single track his mind had been on ever since the Santarian charity ball, he refocused on making sure Alexa made it into his club without incident.

A member of his staff approached her, indicating that he would take her jacket, and Rafe's gut tightened as she slowly pulled at the belt, shrugging her shoulders so that the fabric slipped down her arms.

Rafe nearly choked on the air he'd just sucked into his lungs.

The dress she was wearing was black, tight and minimal in the extreme. It was as if the manufacturer had run out of fabric, shrugged and sewn it together anyway. Sheer gossamer tights covered legs that looked impossibly long in stiletto heels. Her waist looked tiny, her breasts full and voluptuous.

Nearby, men gave her covetous looks and Rafe found himself moving towards the lift that would take him to the ground floor before he'd even thought about it. She would cause a war in his club if he didn't immediately bundle her back into that coat.

'I feel so alive. Almost electric.' Alexa's eyes sparkled with pleasure when she spotted him. 'This place is fantastic. Dark and mysterious— it's as if something magical could happen around any corner. But it's also a touch romantic with the effect of the mauve and blue lighting on the wall murals. And the music—'

Hannah interrupted her excitement with a glass of champagne. 'It's French, of course. You look brilliant. That dress is perfect. Don't you think so, Rafe?'

'Perfect.'

Alexa raised a brow at his droll reply. He was going to have to pull himself together before he sank his hands into all that lustrous hair and said to hell with the club—they were going back to the apartment to have the kind of sex he was always reputed to have.

'Thanks to you, Hannah.' Alexa grinned happily. 'I had the most amazing afternoon.'

'My pleasure,' Hannah replied. 'I'll swap the office for Bond Street any day of the week.'

'Are you okay?' Alexa finally remembered he was present and frowned. 'You seem angry.'

'I'm not angry. But I suggest you don't bend over in that dress.'

'Is it too short? Hannah assured me that it wouldn't stand out in the crowd.'

Rafe gave Hannah a look that promised she'd be missing her bonus next Christmas. 'Hannah was wrong.'

'Okay, well… I think I see a fire I need to put out,' Hannah said tactfully. 'You two have fun.'

Alexa smoothed her hands down the slightly flared hem of her dress. 'It's no shorter than some of the other dresses being worn tonight. I have to confess I didn't think you'd mind, given the photos of some of the women I've seen you with.'

Yes, but none of those women had been his wife, and he had never even noticed if anyone had thrown them admiring glances. Now he couldn't stop noticing the men who cast covetous glances Alexa's way.

'Let's go to my table.'

That would be a safe place to stash her for a while. She could watch everything that happened from the third-floor balcony that overlooked two split-level dance floors before he sent her home.

She pressed in closely behind him, grabbing the sleeve of his shirt so she didn't lose him in the crowd. Rafe thought about placing her in front of him but there was only so much his control could handle, and having her pert derrière so close at hand just might tip him over the edge.

'I know I'm not familiar with nightclubs,' she said as he led her up the circular glass staircase, nodding to one of the ground staff monitoring the third floor, 'but I doubt there would ever be one out there to top this. You must be really proud.'

Exceptionally pleased by her praise, he smiled. 'I'm glad you like it.'

Reaching their destination, he ushered her into the velvet-upholstered circular sofa. Her slender legs were partially concealed by the small central table, but that left her cleavage and her wide, happy smile for him to focus on and that wasn't much better. Forget working out how much time they had left in days, he needed to work out how much time they had left in hours; it would at least give his mind something to do.

One hundred and ninety two.

Not helpful.

Trying to ignore how tense Rafe was wasn't easy, but by her second glass of champagne Alexa was managing it. Berenia didn't have anything like this and while she was used to being the centre of attention she'd never been completely comfortable with it. But here, in this club, she felt as if she could be anyone. She didn't feel as if she had to be the proper Crown Princess. She felt as if she could let her hair down. And she had. The feel of it against her bare back heightened her senses and made her feel so different from her usual self. So did the loud music flooding her body with its throbbing beat.

She glanced across at Rafe, who was speaking to someone who had stopped at their table and who was more interested in him than in her. This was his domain and she liked seeing him in it. She liked taking a back seat. Like this, she could just be any one of the women he took out with him. A woman he would later take home. To his bed.

Her gaze roamed his wide shoulders and silky dark hair. She'd always imagined that her dream man would be someone upstanding and good. Someone like his brother, whom she'd built her secret fantasies around, based on his chivalrous actions when she was younger. But really, the King of Santara, as handsome as he was, had never made her feel the way Rafe did. Never made her want to climb into his lap and straddle his hard thighs the way she wanted to do now.

As if she'd actually reached over and touched him, Rafe turned his head away from the man leaning on their booth seat, his smoky gaze connecting with hers as if he knew every one of her sinfully erotic thoughts. Instinctively, her eyes moved to his sensual mouth and the stubble that had grown in over the course of the day. In a black shirt, his hair falling in thick waves, he looked like a modern-day pirate.

Alexa casually picked up her champagne glass and tried to pretend that her heart wasn't racing. What would he say if she vocalised her desires? What would he say if she slid along the raspberry-coloured bench seat and whispered that she wanted to change their bargain? That she wanted sex with him whether it was meaningless or not.

'I see everyone agrees that this club is sensational,' she said as the man Rafe had been conversing with strolled away from their table. 'You must feel proud.'

'It takes an army of people to create something like this. It's not all my doing.'

'But it takes a visionary to conceive of it, and then someone to take the risk and actually execute it.'

He swallowed a mouthful of champagne and Alexa felt transfixed by the movement of his throat. She felt breathless and the cavernous room seemed to shrink as he sat there watching her with an intensity she wanted to interpret as sexual.

Because this man might be wrong for her on so many levels but that didn't stop her from wanting him. He was so easy to talk to, so easy to be with. It was sexy to be able to say something to a man and have him actually listen to her. And she did feel safe with him. Safe and sensual. Especially when he kissed her.

'Alexa, if you don't stop looking at me like that I'm likely to do something we'll both regret.'

His deep growly voice flowed through her body like hot caramel. 'Like what?'

His blue eyes turned as hot as a flame, his body going so still at her words she knew he was holding his breath. 'Like things you don't want to know about.'

Alexa's tongue slipped out to moisten her dry lips. 'Maybe I do.'

'You don't.' The blunt words were edged in steel and made all the insecurities left over from Stefano, and King Jaeger's, rejection come storming back to her. What was she doing? She wasn't some femme fatale! She was the woman that men walked away from.

But you already know he's going to walk away, a little voice reminded her. *It's why you chose him.*

Emboldened by that voice, her slinky dress and the hard, hot man beside her, Alexa decided she could either give into her inadequacies or throw caution to the wind and see what happened. With her heart in her mouth she embraced the latter, slowly crossing one leg over the other and gathering her hair in one hand to bring it forward over her shoulder. 'Why don't you let me be the judge of what I want? I'm not a child, Rafe.'

'I know you're not a child,' he bit out. 'Nobody looking at you in that dress could mistake you for one.'

'You don't like my dress?'

Before he could respond a laughing Hannah stopped by their table. 'Everything okay, boss?'

'Everything is fine, Hannah. You can officially clock off duty now and have a drink.'

'Oh, thank goodness.' She gave Alexa a wide smile. 'I've been desperate to hit the dance floor. Have you had a dance yet, Your Highness?'

'Please, just call me Alexa. A title seems so inappropriate tonight. Tonight I just want to have fun.'

'Then let's dance. Do you want to come, boss?'

'No.'

'Mind if I drag Alexa along?'

'Yes.'

But Alexa was already sliding from the booth seat. 'Don't listen to him, Hannah. I'd love to go dancing. It's what I'm here for.'

Hannah laughed. 'I like this one. Make sure you don't do anything to lose her.'

Weaving her way down the stairs, Alexa could feel Rafe's gaze on her the whole way but she refused to turn and glance back at him. Somehow she knew the steps to the timeless game he had started playing with her at the Summer Palace, which had stalled when her father had forced them to get married. Well, no one was forcing him to do anything now, and if he didn't want her she'd find someone else who did. After all, that had been the point of her initial mission—to buy herself some time to find a man she *did* want to marry.

Unfortunately, her mind seemed inconveniently stuck on one man right now. *Her Prince.*

'This club is going to be on everyone's list of where to go for years,' Hannah stated, raising her voice above the upbeat music. 'I love my job!'

She waved her hands in the air, her enthusiasm catching, and Alexa found herself loosening up as she gave up any semblance of self-consciousness and moved her body in a way that felt sexy and liberating.

'So you like working for Rafe?' she asked.

'Oh, he's amazing. The best boss in the world. And I'm not just saying that because you're his wife—it's true. He's generous and disciplined and so kind. Last month he asked me to organise an all-expenses-paid holiday to the Caribbean for a month, along with six months off with full pay, for one of our accountants whose wife is ill. He's a dream boss.'

A dream boss? Hannah had just described her dream man. She certainly hadn't described someone Alexa had believed to be self-centred and hedonistic.

'You're a lucky woman to have captured him,' Hannah continued. 'I think a thousand women lay heartbroken in their beds on the day you married.'

'You can stop talking now, Hannah.'

Alexa turned at Rafe's droll tone to find him standing stock-still in front of her, the gyrating bodies of the other dancers surrounding him like caricatures in a stage play. She slowly dropped her arms from over her head, unable to take her eyes from his.

'I thought you didn't want to dance?' Hannah laughed.

'I don't.' Rafe's gaze slid down over Alexa's body with such searing heat she turned liquid inside. 'Go get a drink, Hannah. Your duty is done here.'

'I can see that.' Hannah grinned and melted into the surrounding dancers.

Alexa didn't notice Hannah disappear; she only had eyes for Rafe, who was looking at her as a wolf might look at a helpless deer.

'I do like your dress. But I like you even more.'

'You do?'

His hands moved to the sides of her waist.

'Too much. I've been trying to avoid giving in to this all week, but you've defeated me.' His voice turned low and growly. 'But this won't just blur those lines between us, Princess, it will completely obliterate them.'

'I don't mind.'

A serious glint entered his dark eyes. 'And if it's another mistake?'

'Are you trying to warn me off you? I'm not that naive young girl any more, Rafe. I've grown up a lot since Stefano. I know this isn't about love, so if you're worried that I'll fall for you like every other woman, I won't.'

'That's not what I'm afraid of.'

'Then what are you afraid of?'

His hand came up to the side of her face, his fingers stroking through the heavy strands of her hair. They could have been alone for all the notice they took of the energetic dancers around them. 'I'm afraid I won't want to stop once I've had you. I'm afraid I want you too much.'

His words were thrilling, a balm to her wounded feminine soul. 'Then take me,' she whispered, moving a step closer so that her body was flush up against his. 'Take me and show me what pure, unadulterated pleasure feels like.'

A harsh curse left Rafe's mouth right before his lips crashed down over hers. It was like a match meeting a firecracker. Alexa's body caught alight, her mind empty of everything else but this moment. This man.

Too soon the kiss was over, Rafe lifting his head and tucking her in tightly against him. 'We can't stay here. We'll get arrested.'

All but dragging her from the dance floor, Rafe stopped briefly in front of her security detail before clamping his hand over hers and leading her along a series of narrow hallways until he opened a heavy door and ushered her through.

Glancing around, she realised they were in an underground garage beside a shiny black motorbike.

Rafe pulled out a leather jacket from beneath the seat and fed her arms into it. The jacket swamped her and smelled of him.

'What about you?' she asked when she noticed that there was only one.

'I'm hot enough.'

There were many responses she could make to that but she didn't have the experience or confidence to banter with him in that way.

Rafe pulled a helmet from the handlebars and turned back to her. One of his hands went to her hair and he breathed deeply. 'Your hair is beautiful.' He twisted the strands in his fist and brought her mouth to his in a fierce kiss that set her on fire all over again.

Alexa moaned softly as he released her.

'Home first,' he said, plunking the helmet on her head and buckling it.

Taking his hand, Alexa slid her legs over the back of the bike and settled on the seat, futilely tugging at her skirt. 'Ignore it and hang on tight,' Rafe instructed. 'I won't be going slowly.'

It was a rush to know that she affected him like this and she did what he asked, sliding her arms around his lean waist as the bike started to move.

CHAPTER SEVEN

THE RIDE HOME was as fast as he'd warned it would be. Alexa felt as if she'd just got used to the vibration of the engine between her legs and the thrill of being on a bike for the first time when he was zooming down the slope that led to his underground garage.

Moments later they were in the lift and heading skyward. Rafe watched her from across the small cubicle but didn't touch her. She used the time to catch her breath, her senses completely alert to his every breath.

Stepping out of the lift, Alexa smoothed her skirt and wondered what to do with her hands. Now that she was here, now that they were doing this, she felt a moment's hesitation.

'Alexa?'

Standing before her, all tall, dark and dangerously male, he made her heartbeat quicken. He was so beautiful,, his jaw clenched with the intensity of his arousal.

The knowledge was as intoxicating as it was

scary because, for someone who always thought about the consequences of her actions, Alexa knew she hadn't thought this through completely. She also knew that she might never experience a feeling like this again and that she wanted this man. She wanted him more than was good for her.

'You still with me, princess?'

Rafe smoothed his hands over her shoulders, his touch electric. Alexa's eyes sought his and although she knew this would likely mean more to her than it would to him she couldn't bring herself to care. After she and Rafe ended their marriage she would always have this memory, this moment, and she shoved any remaining inhibitions and concerns aside and took the extra step needed to bring her into his arms.

'Yes,' she husked. 'I'm still with you.'

Taking her at her word Rafe took command, pressing her back against the door and eradicating the last of her doubts with an erotically charged kiss.

It was like a brand, a claim that said 'mine', and Alexa opened her mouth to the demand of his tongue. Her arms went around his neck to hold him close, her fingers buried in his hair as she pulled him closer.

'You smell like sugar and…leather,' he groaned, his lips working their way along her jawline as he swiftly stripped the jacket down her arms and let it drop to the floor.

Excitement poured through her at the hunger in his eyes, her legs suddenly giving out so that the only thing holding her up was his arms, banded around her waist.

He moved his hands to cup her bottom and Alexa moaned indistinctly into his mouth, her body craving his.

Needing to touch his skin, her fingers tugged at his shirt until she had it free, a frisson of desire racing through her as she stroked her fingers over lean male flesh.

Her touch unleashed something primal inside him because his mouth turned greedy and hot, his hard body pinning her to the door as his hands roamed, bringing her core up against his hot hard erection.

'Rafe?' Alexa wrenched her head back as everything inside her softened to yield to that hard male presence between her legs.

Swearing softly, he scooped her into his arms and carried her into his bedroom.

Momentarily breaking the kiss, he slid her body down his until she was standing in front of him. With sure, practised fingers he found the invisible zip in the side of her dress and deftly divested her of both her dress and her bra, holding her hands to the side so that he could look at her.

'You're beautiful,' he breathed, bringing one hand up to cup her breast while the other went to the back of her head to bring her mouth back up to his.

The kiss was fierce and sweet, the sensations of his fingers teasing her nipple sending sparks of need through her body that obliterated everything else except the man touching her.

'Oh, please…' She didn't know what she was begging him to do but when his mouth closed over the tip of her breast and he flicked her with his tongue she thought she might expire from pleasure. Shifting to her other breast, he let out a low chuckle at her soft pleas and then she felt the coolness of the mattress at her back as he lowered her onto it.

Aroused and aching, Alexa fumbled with the buttons on his shirt, desperate to expose his body to her view. Helping her, Rafe shrugged wide shoulders until the shirt slid down his back and her hands roved over his naked chest and back.

The sheer size and power of his corded body was breathtaking and even though part of her knew it was dangerous to want him this much she couldn't help it. She had no control over her body or her senses and she didn't want any. She was a willing captive to the fever raging through her body, and she would have flown into the centre of the sun if he had asked her to.

His lips returned to hers, commanding and potently male, his fingers hot against the inside of her thighs as he swept them higher until he was cupping her through her panties.

A small whimper escaped her and she bit gently into the hard ball of his shoulder as his finger stroked and teased until she was a writhing mass of nerves and sensation.

'Rafe, please...'

Smiling against her neck, he nuzzled at her breast, flicking his tongue against the rigid peak at the same time as his fingers teased.

'Please what, my sweet?' He continued to stroke and torture as he slowly, so slowly, shifted the silk aside until finally he was touching her, his fingers finding and parting her flesh before plunging inside her hot, wet sheath.

Gripped in a fever of desire, Alexa wasn't sure who groaned the loudest and then she didn't care as Rafe expertly flicked a finger across the bundle of nerves nested at her apex and sent her spiralling into an earth-shattering orgasm that made her scream.

She must have lost consciousness because suddenly her panties were gone and Rafe had cupped her bottom and raised her to his lips, his tongue lapping at her and bringing her body to another mind-numbing climax.

Spent and gasping, she couldn't move as Rafe

crawled back up her body, kissing every inch of skin he came into contact with.

'You,' Rafe growled, coming down over her with lethal male grace, 'are incredible.'

Alexa felt incredible but she wanted more. The space between her legs felt hollow and empty, her eyes widening as Rafe rose to his knees and unzipped his trousers. With bated breath she watched as he lowered the fabric down over his hips, his thick, gorgeous erection springing free.

Unaware that she'd licked her lips until he made a low growly sound, she pushed to a sitting position and ran her hands down over his heated torso, the dark hair on his chest soft like a wolf's pelt beneath her fingers. Moving downwards, she couldn't stop herself from reaching out to touch him. As she gripped him her eyes flew to his. He'd sunk his teeth into his lower lip, his eyes hooded as he watched her, and it made her more daring.

Stroking firmly, she felt one of his hands softly grip her hair and she hadn't even realised she'd brought her mouth closer to the swollen length of him until she felt him against her lips.

The earthy taste of him burst across her tongue, the flavour so deeply male. She opened her lips and took him into her mouth, a heady sense of power filling her when his fingers gripped harder in her hair and a groan tore from his throat.

Loving the silky hard length of him against her tongue, Alexa increased the pressure of her lips until she heard him swear, and then she was being pulled up and stretched out beneath him like a feast.

A thrill raced through her as he parted her thighs and looked down at her. Grabbing a condom from the side table drawer, he rolled it on and then braced himself with his hands either side of her face. Mesmerised, Alexa couldn't look away from his hungry gaze as he slowly pushed into her.

Something in the way he watched her almost tenderly made her unable to tear her eyes from his. Rafe must have felt the force of the connection too because his lips came down to claim hers once more as his body thrust hard, filling her and driving her to the heights of another pulse-pounding climax before he followed her over the edge on a hoarse cry of completion.

Waking up from what might actually have been the best sex of his life, Rafe glanced at the woman curled up in his arms, her dark hair spread out on his white sheets like a waterfall of black silk. She was asleep, her head nestled in the curve of his shoulder and her sweet breath warm against his chest.

Waiting for the usual need for space and privacy to overtake him, he was surprised when it didn't come. Instead he felt replete and relaxed, and more complete than he'd felt in forever.

Complete?

The alien concept entered his head then was gone just as quickly. Sex didn't make him feel complete. That wasn't what he was feeling. What he was feeling was… It was… He frowned. It was pure, unadulterated pleasure after a week of being tied up in the tightest sexual knots he'd ever experienced.

No woman had ever made him want so much or had satisfied him so fully.

Had he really thought he'd be able to ignore her, with the level of sexual chemistry they shared? Well, if he had, he couldn't now. Alexa had been responsive and giving and so sweet that just the memory of her hands and mouth on his body was turning him surprisingly hard again.

His hands stroked down over the silky skin of her arm, his fingers finding and twining with hers. She breathed out a sigh and relaxed more deeply against his side.

He remembered that she'd been up working late last night and was probably exhausted. She worked hard and took her job seriously. Which he supposed she had to. Just as seriously as he took his. When you had the amount of staff he had relying on you to provide their wages it was important to perform well. He supposed they were similar that way. Only he no longer sought the approval of others the way he suspected Alexa did. He'd given up on needing to please a long time ago. She would need to do that too once she became Queen or she'd work herself into the ground. But why was he thinking about Alexa's future?

Usually he didn't concern himself with a woman's life after sex. He'd already moved onto his next task or his next project. It didn't matter where he was, or who the woman was, Rafe always liked to be on the move, rarely staying still long enough to feel trapped. It came, he knew, from always having to toe the royal line when he was younger. From having a father who'd demanded that he behave a certain way, and then giving him grief if he missed the mark.

But why waste time thinking about things that weren't important when he had a warm naked woman he knew would be receptive to his advances if he were to wake her with a soft kiss on those delectable lips?

At least he assumed she'd be receptive. Every other woman he'd ever been with would be, but Alexa wasn't like every other woman. She didn't play the same games, acting coy to try to attract his attention, or turning girlish when she had it. Alexa was far too straightforward and earnest.

But then she had no need to play games with him because they were already married. She already had his ring on her finger and he had hers on his.

He held his hand up to the moonlight that spilled in through the gap in the curtains. The room was too dark for him to see the gold, but he could just make out the dull shape of the band. When she'd first slipped it on his finger the weight had felt foreign and unwanted. Funny how it didn't feel like that any more.

It felt right and good.

Right and good?

Something stirred behind his breastbone, some unwanted emotion that caused his ribs to tighten around his chest.

As if sensing his unease, Alexa shifted her knee higher across his thigh. A shot of lust raced through him, a primitive hunger that bordered on need.

Not that he did need. Need had a serious edge of permanence about it. Want? Now want was something he understood. It came and went and put a smile on his face, and his body stirred at the way he *wanted* to wake Alexa now with a line of slow kisses starting at her slender shoulder and encompassing her whole body.

Shifting again, she made a cute little sleep sound that made him lose his train of thought.

He felt her body tense as she awoke and he

gently gathered her closer, stroking his hand down the silky skin of her spine.

'Stay asleep, Princess,' he murmured, even though sleep was the last thing on his mind. 'I know you're tired.'

'Sleep?' She raised her head and blinked at him. 'I...' She looked flustered, her eyes uncertain in the dim light as she stared at his face, his chest.

Her tongue came out to lick her lips and before he was even aware that he'd made the decision he rolled her onto her back and kissed her.

After a split second of hesitation her arms went around his neck, her body rising to his.

Hunger ripped through him at the soft sound of pleasure she made when he stroked his tongue into her mouth, his body primed to take her immediately.

But he also wanted to savour her. He wanted to taste her body again, her sweetness.

Loving the way she clung to him, Rafe kissed his away across her face. First her cheeks and the soft skin below her ears, then her eyelids and her nose. Feeling her completely relax beneath him, he slowly moved down her body, laving her neck and licking at her collarbone.

Her gorgeous breasts pointed skyward, her nipples achingly beautiful, and he took first one and then the other into his mouth. Then he positioned her so that she was beneath him, her long legs moving restlessly on the outside of his own.

He used his knees to open her to the hard throb of his erection and he sank into her softness with unerring accuracy. She sobbed his name as he slowly filled her, sweat beading his forehead as her body took him in, her inner muscles gripping him tight.

'Alexa…' he groaned, remembering at the last minute that he wasn't wearing a condom. She arched beneath him, her lower body straining for his thrust.

Seriously perturbed at just how close he had come to forgetting protection, he reached into his side table and sheathed himself before thrusting back inside her tight body.

She came almost instantly, the hot pulsing sensation of her climax shattering his self-control in a maelstrom of pleasure.

Opening her eyes to find herself wrapped in Rafe's arms for the second time that morning, Alexa felt herself tense at the overwhelming vulnerability of being naked in his arms. Not because she regretted what they'd shared, but because she liked it a little too much. The feeling left her somehow defenceless, and her instinct was to pull back because, while she had anticipated the pleasure, she hadn't counted on the emotional connection she'd feel when he joined his body with hers. Only she was quite sure Rafe would have experienced no such thing in return.

Undoubtedly last night had been par for the course for a man of his experience, and she had to keep that front and centre in her mind at all times. Because while she had experienced something monumental in his bed, she knew she'd be alone in that line of thinking.

But it had been monumental. The way he had worshipped her body, the tender kisses he'd lavished on her, the powerful thrusts of his body... It had definitely been mind-blowing, but not in the way that he had meant it would be. It was mind-blowing in that it was so lovely. So beautiful. So everything.

Deeply asleep, he was sprawled on his side, one arm above his head, the other draped over her waist. Shifting slightly out from under his hold, Alexa took advantage of the moment to take her fill of him.

Naked, he was utterly superb. The swell of his biceps and muscled shoulders, the broad chest and trail of hair that bisected his flat belly, the lean line of his hip that made her want to put her lips on his skin again.

He'd lost none of his power or authority in sleep, but he did look more peaceful. More rested. She thought about the things she had discov-

ered about him the night before. His generosity
with his employees, his strong work ethic and the
way his employees treated him with such deference and respect. Hannah had sung his praises
and not because he was a prince. She truly liked
and admired him for the man that he was.

A man, Alexa was starting to suspect, was
decent and kind, even though she doubted he'd
admit to it. And why was that? Why did he hide
that side of his nature? And why, if he wanted her
so much, had he stayed away from her all week?

Was it out of deference to her wishes? Because
he was afraid she'd fall in love with him? Or
something else? Whatever his reasons, Alexa accepted that she'd been very short-sighted in be-
lieving everything she'd read about him. And
really she should have known better, but then
almost everyone believed what had been written about him and he didn't help that by not de-
fending himself.

Still, there was no doubting some of the stories.
He was a notorious playboy, and he'd definitely
been a rebel when he was younger—the story
of him stealing his father's favourite sports car
and cruising through the mountains with a girl,
and another of him winning a dangerous cross-
country horse race his father had forbidden him
to enter, and the stories of his wild parties at the
Summer Palace were the stuff of legend—but

there was another side to him. A deeper side she longed to explore further.

Her eyes drifted to his mouth and her body flushed with remembered pleasure at all the ways he'd satisfied her throughout the night. He'd certainly delivered on his promise of unadulterated pleasure and in one night he'd completely obliterated her first bumbling sexual experience with the treacherous Stefano.

Recalling how easily she'd fallen under the Italian's spell all those years ago, even knowing that she was older now, still made her throat constrict with unwanted emotion.

The earlier vulnerability she'd felt on waking in Rafe's arms returned full force, along with the sense that she'd never felt such a soul-deep connection with another human being before.

And that was exactly the kind of thinking she needed to avoid at all costs.

Driven out of bed by the knowledge that she was at risk of history repeating itself and creating meaning where there was none, Alexa quietly made her way to her room and jumped in the shower.

Once there she groaned softly as the soapy cloth moved over the sensitive marks left behind by Rafe's love making. He'd been both tender and demanding during the night, and a smile curved her lips as she thought about the way one particular mark had been formed. Warning herself again not to get hung up on what had happened between them, she pulled on her kimono-style robe and went in search of a much-needed coffee.

Determined to figure out how to work the machine on her own this time, she'd just tried her fourth combination of buttons when she heard a deep chuckle behind her. 'For a smart woman, that machine seems to have defeated you.'

Alexa glanced over her shoulder to find six foot three of hot muscular man leaning against the doorframe watching her. He'd put on baggy sweatpants, the rest of him completely bare, his biceps bulging as he folded his arms across his chest, amusement shining from his sexy blue eyes.

She gave him a droll look, unable to stop her gaze from falling to his naked chest. 'For a man with a huge wardrobe, you seem to have forgotten your shirt.'

A sensual grin curved his mouth as he sauntered towards her. 'Why cover up what you like to look at so much?'

'So arrogant,' she accused, catching her breath when he wrapped his arms around her from behind and nuzzled her neck.

'Why didn't you wake me before you got up?' he murmured, his hot breath making her melt.

'I didn't want to disturb you,' she said. Nor

had she wanted him to spot the panic that had galvanised her out of his arms.

His lips grazed her ear and he gave it a light nip. 'Next time you wake me, okay?'

'But you were sleeping so peacefully.'

'Wake me so I can kiss you good morning.'

Cupping her jaw, he turned her face so that he could demonstrate and Alexa sighed as she leant into him, a sharp pang darting through her as she wondered if he always insisted on morning kisses from his women.

Reluctantly breaking the kiss, he reached around her to change the coffee settings before pressing Start.

'Does this mean you haven't had coffee all week?' he asked, grinning down at her.

'No, it means your very helpful concierge has brought me one from the café next door every morning.'

He turned her in his arms and linked his arms around her lower back. 'Now you have me.'

The tender words made Alexa's heart beat faster. If she could stop time this second she would, with his strong arms enfolding her body and his hot gaze pinned to hers.

The tone signalled that her coffee was ready, and severed the connection between them. Alexa rubbed her hands over her arms and gripped the

MICHELLE CONDER   173

mug he handed her in both hands, inhaling the heavenly aroma with a sigh.

Rafe's fingers sifted through her hair, making the mass tumble down around her shoulders.

'This should never be restrained,' he murmured, winding it around his hand.

'It's not practical to wear it down.'

'Practical is boring.'

He dropped a kiss on her mouth before stepping back to grab his own coffee. Alexa watched the play of muscles over his back from beneath the sweep of her lashes, heat curling through her.

When he turned back and saw her a pulse of raw sexual energy arced between them. Watching his eyes darken, a thrill of excitement wound through her right before her stomach announced that it was empty, the loud rumble echoing off the polished angles of the cabinets.

Mortified, she clamped her hand over the offending area and gave him a startled look.

Rafe laughed. 'Aren't princesses allowed to make bodily noises?'

'Not in company.'

'Company?' His eyes narrowed. 'I'm not company.' He dropped his empty espresso cup in the sink and leant back against it, reaching for her and tugging her between his splayed legs. 'I'm your husband.' He massaged the nape of her neck and she moaned as she leant into his touch. 'And your lover. I get special privileges.'

She knew she liked the sound of his words more than was good for her but for some reason she couldn't bring herself to pull away. Being with a man like this was new and intoxicating, and somehow being with *this* man quadrupled the sensation.

'Like hearing my stomach growl?' she said dubiously.

'Like taking you out for breakfast. In fact, let's make it the whole day. We can start with this great place I know that does a mean English breakfast, and play tourist for the day. Go to those places you didn't get to during the week.'

'Really?' Her eyes sparkled like a child standing in front of Harrods' window display at Christmas. Then she remembered that she'd promised to email HR with the report she'd been working on the last few days. 'I would love that but I can't. I have work to finish up.'

'No, you don't. Not only do you need to rest, but it's Saturday.'

'Oh, so it is.' She grinned at him. 'I've lost track of time, and I *never* lose track of time.'

'You work too hard. And while I respect your dedication, you also need to know when to take time out for yourself.'

'And you're going to tell me that now is that

time?' Not waiting for his reply and having thrown caution to the wind once already, she decided that she might as well go all-out. 'Okay, fine. The report I have to finish up isn't all that urgent and this...' she opened her eyes wide '... being here with you, is a rare treat. Will we go there on your bike?'

He laughed at the hopeful note in her voice. 'You liked the bike, huh?'

She gave him a wicked grin. 'I loved the bike. Especially when you did that corner thing where it dipped low.'

'The lean-in.' Setting his hands to her waist, he pulled her closer. 'I love that you love my bike.' He kissed her long and deep, making her body quicken.

Desire consumed her in a flame of need and she moaned, threading her fingers into his hair and flattening her body against his. Rafe made an indistinct sound that was somewhere between pain and pleasure, his hands on the sash of her robe. 'If this goes any further we won't make it out of the apartment.'

'Oh, then we have to stop.'

Stepping back, Alexa retied the sash on her kimono and smoothed her hair.

Rafe shook his head. 'Tossed aside for a hunk of metal. Nice to know.'

Alexa gave him a teasing smile. 'It is a really big hunk of metal, though…'

He reached for her to give her a punishing kiss but she danced out of the way, laughing as he threatened retribution for her impudence.

Breakfast was as large and decadent as he'd promised and afterwards Alexa didn't think she'd be able to eat for a week.

Rafe teased her for her measly attempt and hoovered up her remaining eggs and spinach as if he hadn't just devoured a plate twice the size of hers.

The café he'd taken her to was warm and low-key, like she suspected he liked to live his life. Exactly the opposite to how she lived hers, which was all polished silver service and structured decorum.

Tossing money onto the table, Rafe took her hand and led her from the café as if they were just a normal London couple enjoying a springtime weekend on the town.

Throwing his leg over the big black bike, Rafe kicked the stand up and helped Alexa settle herself on the back, her body automatically moulding to his. He'd given her his leather jacket again and she curled her fingers into the overlong sleeves for extra warmth and tucked them against his stomach. The cool spring temperature wasn't so bad with the visor covering her, but she didn't really care about the cold anyway. She was just enjoying being with Rafe.

'Where to now?'

'I don't know. You decide,' she said, wrapping her arms around his waist as the bike moved off from the kerb.

Rafe was an exceptional driver, his movements smooth and confident as he navigated his way through the congested city streets. But then he was exceptional at most things. His business enterprises, his coffee-making—okay, that was mostly the machine, but still—his dancing, and most of all his love-making…

Hugging him tight, she stopped daydreaming and tuned into the world-famous landmarks that dotted the city. Rafe was clearly enjoying his new role as tour guide, but her attention was more on the man she was wrapped around than anything else.

Until the bike zipped past a relatively normal-looking building bursting with pedestrians and shoppers. Tapping him on the shoulder, Alexa indicated that she wanted him to stop and when she saw that it was a bustling market she clapped her hands with glee.

Ever since she was a young girl she'd been enthralled by the sights and scents of a busy market, loving the combination of old and new, and the anticipation that came with finding a hidden treasure. She still had the pair of lurid green sunglasses her father had once given in and purchased for her on a trip she had tagged along on and, much to Sol's disgust, she'd worn them constantly for months afterwards.

Rafe groaned good-naturedly when he realised how keen she was to explore, swapping their helmets for two caps and tucking her hair out of the way.

'Don't make eye contact with anyone and don't leave my side. I don't feel like getting into a fight.'

Alexa rolled her eyes. They might have left their security detail behind for the day but she'd never felt safer—or happier. Shelving that unsettling thought, she rolled her eyes. 'As if.'

'Sweetheart, with those exotic green eyes of yours I'm almost tempted to keep you indoors.'

Alexa grinned at him; she couldn't help it. 'Compliments like that will get you kissed.'

'In that case, you're not only beautiful inside and out, but when you slid down my stomach earlier and put your mouth on—'

'Rafe!' Knowing exactly what he was about to say, Alexa laughed and reached up to kiss him. His mouth immediately turned hungry and desire coursed through her with unnerving force.

Moaning into his mouth, she extricated herself

from his arms and stepped back. Being with him like this, so relaxed and natural, had a freeing effect on her. It was as if all her fears and inhibitions had been washed away and she didn't have to worry about what the future might bring. It was just the two of them here and now.

'Come on.' She broke the kiss and hooked her arm through his. She'd stashed some pounds in her pocket on her way out of the apartment and she wanted to spend the lot.

Wandering past various vendors, Alexa soaked up the Reggae music and the delightful fragrance of the multicultural food on offer, stopping first to buy some exquisite chocolates and then to stand behind a crowd of onlookers to watch a curly-haired Australian juggler ply his trade.

Later, pleasantly exhausted and dressed in one of Rafe's shirts and a thick pair of socks, Alexa wandered into the kitchen to find Rafe putting the finishing touches to their evening meal.

'He cooks, he rides a motorbike *and* runs a multinational corporation.' She took a glass of Sauterne he held out for her. 'Is there anything you can't do?'

'Concentrate for any length of time when you're in the room.'

'I can live with that.' Alexa laughed because she was meant to, but a pang of longing she didn't expect to feel pierced her heart.

Careful, she warned herself. *You only have seven days left.*

'So what are we having?'

'Steak with pepper sauce, potatoes and salad.'

'Wow, now I'm even more impressed.'

Rafe smiled across the bench at Alexa, unsure if he'd ever enjoyed a woman's company as much as he was enjoying hers. She was bright, funny, beautiful... His eyes took in her clean face and laughing eyes. He liked being with her like this, relaxed, natural, just the two of them without any outside interruptions. And as much as he enjoyed making love with her, having her in his space filled him with a sense of wellbeing he would be hard pressed to explain. Maybe it was knowing that he could take her to bed any time he wanted. Because he did want to. All the time.

'I know that look,' she said huskily, her eyes growing heavy.

'You should.' Rafe told himself to pull it together before she accused him of having a one-track mind.

'So how is it you can cook?' she asked, reaching for a carrot stick.

Glad to be focusing on something else other than the way he was *feeling*, Rafe sliced vegetables and answered her question. 'When I moved to Cambridge I shared a house with a few other guys who could barely reheat beans. Since I had developed a penchant for fine dining, thanks to the palace chef, it was either learn to cook or starve.'

'I'm sure your brother would have provided a chef if you'd asked.'

'He would have, but I was determined to make my own way. Which I did. Partying, drinking, studying…playing darts. You do realise that your lover is a Cambridge darts champion?'

'Darts?' Alexa grinned. 'Be still my beating heart.'

Rafe arched a brow. 'Some respect, please. It's more difficult than it looks.'

Alexa grinned and sipped her wine. 'It sounds like fun. By contrast, I had private tutors and then I studied at Berenia University, surrounded by security.'

He looked up from chopping herbs for the vinaigrette. 'No partying for the future Queen?'

'No.' She gave a wistful sigh. 'I was accepted into an American university, actually. Sol helped me apply and then, when I got in, he managed to convince my father to let me study abroad, but then I made the mistake with…'

Rafe stopped chopping, noting the way the smile had died on her face. 'The Italian with the arms?' he prompted softly.

'Yes. Him. My father decided that I was too

young. Too *vulnerable* to be that far away from home. He was probably right.'

'He wasn't right, Princess, and you need to stop feeling guilty about it. What happened wasn't your fault. You're entitled to make mistakes, and you have to live your life.'

'Yes, but I should have known better. I should have been prepared.'

Hearing the subtle anguish in her voice, Rafe reached over and took her chin gently in his hand. 'How could you? You were seventeen years old. I bet your father kept you under a tight leash when you were young—there, I see I'm right—so what previous experiences could you have had to prepare you for being conned by a man like that?'

She looked at him for so long he wondered if he had offended her when her lips twisted into a faint smile. 'Do you know, when I was in my teens I used to be a champion horsewoman and I always trusted my judgement. Then Stefano happened and *bam*—it's like I've second-guessed myself ever since. I've blamed myself for what happened for so long. Trying to be good and to do the right thing...' Her smile hit him like a sunbeam. 'Why did I never look at it the way you just did?'

Rafe leaned over and gave her a quick, deep kiss before handing her another carrot stick. 'Too hard on yourself, perhaps.'

'Maybe. It's something I've never been able to talk about with anyone else before.' She palmed her glass of wine and watched him cook. 'You're a good listener. And a good person, you know that?'

Rafe placed the steaks on the grill. 'Careful, I'll get a big head.'

'You don't like me saying that.' She tilted her head as she studied him. 'Why not?'

'I suppose I'm not used it. It wasn't something I heard growing up.'

'Your parents never told you that you were a good person?'

'My father and I never saw eye to eye. He told me he'd disown me if I didn't follow his rules.'

'But that's awful.'

'He was hard on all of us. We got used to it.' Rafe shrugged off her sympathy. He never let himself indulge in weak emotions like sympathy and need. 'Do you eat mushrooms?'

'Yes.' She frowned thoughtfully. 'I do remember hearing he was often upset with you, but you were always blamed for any issues that came up.'

Rafe laughed, turning the steaks. 'Often I deserved it.' He gave her his trademark smile, but somehow it felt false. 'I enjoyed riling my father by getting into scraps I shouldn't have.'

'At least he didn't actually follow through on

the threat. I can't imagine how you would have felt if he'd actually disowned you.'

'I have no doubt that he would have, had he lived. Do you want your potatoes salted?'

'Yes, fine,' she dismissed with a wave of her hand. 'And your mother? She didn't tell you that you were a good person either?'

Wondering how the topic of conversation had turned from her to him so neatly, Rafe frowned. He had already told Alexa more about himself than he'd told anyone else and now he was flooded with memories he'd rather forget.

'My mother had her own problems,' he said tonelessly. 'Namely my father. They were always at each other's throats about something or other and I'm not sure she noticed any of us most of the time. She left when I was ten.'

He placed the steaks and potatoes on a plate and dressed the salad.

'Ten?'

He saw the sympathy on Alexa's face and his gut clenched. He still remembered waking up the morning after his mother had stolen out of the palace like a thief in the night, never to return. He'd come to terms with his childhood loss a long time ago. Come to terms with the fact that his mother lived the life of a recluse now, and rarely saw anyone.

'Did you see her often after she left?'

'No. She moved to Europe and Jag, Milena and I stayed in Santara. She didn't want us to go with her. She wanted a clean break, to be able to make a fresh start with her life.'

'But how could a mother do that?'

'Not all women are maternal, Princess.' He held two plates up with a flourish. 'Let's eat.'

Alexa was so shocked by Rafe's revelations about his childhood that she didn't know where to put the information.

According to stories she had heard about her own mother, she had been kind and compassionate, and Alexa would give anything to have memories of her, whereas Rafe sounded like he'd give anything *not* to have memories of his.

Her heart went out to him as a young boy stuck in a volatile household. Hers hadn't been overly warm, her father often a distant figure, but she'd never doubted his love for her.

'But what about Milena and Jaeger?' she asked, following him to the table. 'Did it bring you closer to them?' Because she had always run to Sol when she'd felt down, and she missed him terribly now that he was gone.

'Yes and no. Milena was extremely young when our mother left and she needed a lot of support. Jag was away at boarding school.' He set their wine glasses on the table. 'I hope you're hungry.'

She was starving but she didn't care about food. 'Do you ever talk about it with Jag or Milena?' she prodded.

The look he gave her was one of surprise. 'Why would I do that? They have their lives, and I have mine.'

'It might be healthy,' she offered. 'How do you know they're not suffering in some way?'

She saw a muscle pulsing in his jaw as if she'd hit a nerve, his eyes suddenly remote. 'Jag and Milena both have my number if they need me. And you——' he said with silky emphasis '——do not need to concern yourself with any of this. I'm fine, Alexa. There's nothing missing from my life.'

What about love? she thought.

He didn't have love, but nor did he want it. As soon as the thought entered her mind a deep sense of misery filled her whole body. Misery for the boy whose parents had cared more about their own needs than those of their children. And misery at the wounds their behaviour had inflicted—inadvertent or otherwise. But at least now she had some understanding as to why he was the way he was.

Where she had always craved connection to others as a result of the lack of warmth in her own childhood—often to her personal detriment— Rafe had been let down by the very people who should have had his back, so he didn't let anyone close. He didn't try at all.

And she would do well to remember that because he didn't want that to change, and she'd be a fool to want it to be otherwise.

CHAPTER EIGHT

SOMETHING TICKLED HER ribs and Alexa swatted at it. 'Don't wake me.'

'I thought you were a morning person.'

She rolled over and groaned when she saw the clock. 'I am when I've managed to get some sleep.'

Rafe sat down on the bed beside her. 'I have coffee.'

'Coffee?' Alexa sprang up and blinked the sleep from her eyes. She breathed deeply and there it was, that delicious aroma.

Rafe laughed and handed her a mug. 'So predictable. But drink up. I have a surprise for you.'

'You do?'

'How do you feel about going on a road trip?'

'Don't you have to work?'

'Hannah's been nagging me about taking time off so I've cancelled my appointments for the next couple of days. If you need any further incentive, the road trip involves my bike.'

'It does?' Feeling helplessly happy and knowing it was dangerous to keep indulging in an emotion that had everything to do with the man creating it, Alexa shelved the voice in her head that said she was letting herself feel too much and nodded. 'Give me five minutes.'

Rafe laughed, leaning in to give her a lingering kiss. 'Now I really am jealous of my bike.'

A couple stretched into five days of exploring the English and Scottish countryside, as well as each other.

Rafe had taken her to Cambridge and the pub he'd frequented during his student days. From there they'd spent an afternoon climbing the ruggedly green Old Man of Coniston in the Lake District, before skipping over the border to explore Scotland. They'd stopped at Glasgow for a few nights where Rafe had checked out the nightclub scene and a couple of buildings he said he was thinking of investing in. One in particular, a grand old Art Deco cinema, Alexa had fallen in love with, totally on board with his vision of restoring it to its former glory rather than tearing it down.

Now they were by Loch Ness, standing under a cloudy sky and staring at the inky black waters of the lake.

'I've always wanted to see the monster,' Alexa said, her eyes searching for a tell-tale ripple or sign of an arched neck.

Rafe slipped his open coat around her body and hugged her closer against the sudden drop in the temperature. 'There is no monster.'

'Don't ruin the fun of it.' She burrowed even further into him against the cold. 'I've decided I'm going to do this every year.'

'Look for the Loch Ness monster?'

'No.' She jabbed him playfully. 'Take off for a week where no one knows who I am or where I am. I might even get my motorbike licence.'

'The Princess who rides?'

'Absolutely.'

She tilted her head up to gaze into his amused blue eyes. They stayed like that for what felt like an eternity, the connection between them so deep it took her breath away more than the scenery.

Suddenly feeling something damp on her face, Alexa shifted her gaze to the sky. 'Rafe! It's snowing!'

He smiled at her indulgently, stroking a flake from her cheek. 'So it is. Rare for this time of year, but damn cold enough!'

She started laughing and turned out of the circle of his arms to spread hers wide. 'I've never seen snow before. It's glorious.'

'You're glorious.' He pulled her back to him and crushed her lips beneath his until she forgot all about the snow.

When they finally parted to draw breath Rafe

reached down to brush the wetness from her cheeks. 'Happy?'

Alexa could have melted into a contented puddle at the way he was looking at her. 'So happy.'

The following morning, their last on the road, Alexa relaxed in the quaint bedroom of a traditional English pub somewhere in a picturesque valley in the Yorkshire Dales.

It was dreamily quiet and she had woken to the faint sound of birds outside her window, and a crisp layer of snow covering the valley. Snuggled up in bed, she realised that she hadn't practised her normal yoga routine or thought about work all week, and she didn't even care. This trip with Rafe was a break from real life and she'd embraced it much more heartily than she would have thought possible.

Out here, they were just Mr and Mrs Nobody, taking a week off and travelling together. Last night the publican and his wife hadn't batted an eye as they'd pulled up late and asked if they had a room. A week ago Alexa would never have thought she would ever be in such a situation. She'd never thought she'd feel this magical, and all because she'd decided to 'take charge', as he'd suggested, and embraced uncertainty.

She could only imagine Nasrin's face when she told her how sexy the Prince really was. Or would she tell her? She'd certainly grown close to Nasrin over the last three years, but perhaps this experience was too private to share with anyone. Because she had no doubt that Nasrin would have her romantic hat on and interrogate her with a litany of questions about what had happened and how she felt about him. No doubt expecting Alexa to have fallen in love with him or something equally absurd.

Fortunately she wasn't at risk of that happening. She was having a good time with Rafe. A wonderful time, but that was all it was for both of them. The public might have bought their romantic love story but Alexa knew the truth, and this time she was determined to remain objective.

Wondering why she felt so unsettled all of a sudden, she nearly fell on the phone beside the bed as it started to ring. Out of habit she picked it up, checking the display before she realised that it was Rafe's phone and not her own.

Regan's name flashed across the screen and Alexa glanced at the bathroom door, where she could hear the shower running. She'd been too drowsy to join Rafe when he'd tried to cajole her into shower sex, promising to go in search of a soy latte for her as soon as he was out.

Regan's name flashed again and Alexa sat up, pulling Rafe's discarded T-shirt over her head to ward off the chill, and swiped the screen to answer the call. The Queen might be calling because of a family emergency and she didn't feel comfortable letting it go through to voicemail when she had the chance to answer it.

Delighted to hear her voice, Regan was keen to find out how Alexa was enjoying her time in England with Rafe and, before she knew it, Alexa found herself drawn in by the other woman's natural warmth. It was clear why the King had fallen in love with her. Even on the phone she was animated and sincere, so opposite to Alexa's own tendency to be closed down. Not that she'd been closed down this week. In fact the way she'd been with Rafe shocked the life out of her. Reminding her that she could be fun and relaxed when she wasn't so worried about the future, and how everyone perceived her.

Maybe a little bit of Rafe's capacity to let things go had rubbed off on her. Not that she'd go as far as he had in letting things go. Like letting go of his country, and his family.

'So I've organised a surprise birthday dinner for Jag in London tomorrow night,' Regan said in a hushed tone as if she half expected her husband to sneak up behind her. 'And I haven't heard yet if Rafe is coming. It's not that big a deal because I've booked the whole restaurant, but I'd really like to know. It would mean so much to Jag and me if you were both there.'

'Of course we'll be there,' Alexa said, not really thinking about the ramifications of that statement until she hung up and Rafe strolled out of the shower a couple of minutes later, a white towel draped around his lean hips, another draped around his shoulders, the tips of his hair glistening with wet drops from the shower.

'She lives.' He grinned at her. 'I was hoping you'd join me.'

'I was thinking about it,' she murmured, automatically opening her mouth for his kiss. 'But then Regan rang.'

Given that he'd said that he liked things just the way they were between him and his siblings, she wasn't sure how to tell him she'd accepted Regan's invitation. She would give anything to be able to go to another birthday dinner for Sol but she knew that Rafe didn't feel the same way about his family.

Rafe dropped the towel from around his shoulders, going still. 'Is everything okay?'

'Everything's fine. She told me she's throwing your brother a surprise birthday party tomorrow night and that you haven't RSVP'd.'

Rafe nuzzled a path down the side of her neck. 'I've been so distracted I forgot. I need to let her know that we're busy.'

Alexa braced her hands on the balls of his shoulders to shift him back.

'Are we busy?'

He frowned as she thwarted his attempt to rid her of his T-shirt. 'Yes. Tomorrow is our last night before you return to Berenia and I plan to make love with you the entire time.'

Their last night together? How had it come about so quickly? And how had she forgotten?

'Would you mind terribly if we had a slight change in plan?' she asked, arching her neck as he resumed his teasing kisses.

'How slight?'

'Well…' She winced, some sixth sense warning her that this might not go as well as she'd originally hoped. 'I sort of accepted Regan's invitation on your behalf.'

As predicted, Rafe drew back, frowning at her. 'How do you sort of accept an invitation?'

'You say yes.'

'Why would you do that?'

'Because it's a *really* nice idea, and she *really* wants you to be there. She said it would make Jag's night.'

Rafe shook his head, moving further away from her. 'I just saw my brother at our wedding two weeks ago, and then at the ball two weeks before that. I've seen him more this month than I did the whole of last year.'

'Surely that's all the more reason to go.' Sensing his physical and emotional withdrawal, and hating it, Alexa touched his arm. 'What are you afraid of?'

'Afraid of?' Rafe barked out a laugh. 'Fear isn't what's keeping me from wanting to go.'

'Then what is? Because it's important to make time for family.'

'Not all family members are best friends, Alexa.'

'I know. Which is why it's so vital to forge strong bonds. The more you see someone, the more you want to see them.'

Rafe gave her a look. 'Sometimes the opposite occurs.'

'It doesn't count with family because, as annoying as they can be, they're the only ones who will rush to your side when the chips are down.'

'I don't plan to let my chips go anywhere,' he drawled. 'Especially not down.'

Alexa returned his look of a moment ago and pushed a skein of her hair back behind her shoulders. Rafe's eyes darkened, the air between turning from frigid to molten in a matter of seconds.

'You did that deliberately,' he accused softly.

Dragging air into her lungs, Alexa blinked. 'Did what?'

'Doesn't matter. It won't work.'

Their eyes locked and then he vaulted off the bed, turning his back on her to stare out of the small window.

The morning had brightened and the sunlight drew shadows across his muscular shoulders and biceps, the white towel riding low on his lean hips. Alexa knew she had crossed a line in accepting the Queen's invitation on his behalf; she'd known it at the time, and she should never have done it. Not that she had expected his complete withdrawal or the hollow feeling inside her chest as if someone had carved out her heart and left an empty cavity behind.

'I'm sorry.' She moved towards him and placed her hand in the centre of his back, enthralled with the play of muscle that bunched beneath the surface of his skin at her touch. 'That was incredibly arrogant of me to impose my ideas of family onto you. I absolutely hate it when people think that they know better about my life than I do and I should have spoken to you first.'

Rafe swung around, his eyes full of an emotion that was somewhere between pain and anger, and she couldn't move. In the distance she heard the tread of someone's footsteps as they walked past their room and the sound of crockery clinking together, but all she could focus on was Rafe standing before her like a Greek God come to life.

He made a rough sound in the back of his throat and then his hands were in her hair, tugging her up onto her toes so that her lips were inches from his. 'How can I resist you when you look at me like this?' His voice was rough, his mouth hard and insistent when it met hers, his kiss eradicating everything else in the world for her but him. This man who gave new meaning to her life.

Alexa moaned, her mouth opening beneath his in an emotional onslaught of need that seemed never-ending, her hands clinging to his wide shoulders as if she might tumble over a cliff and be dashed against jagged rocks if she were to let him go.

Finally Rafe raised his head, leaning his forehead against hers, his breathing ragged.

'I'll go to my brother's party. This time. But, even though I know you mean well, I don't want you to ever interfere with my relationship with my family again. It is what it is, and I can't change that. I don't *want* to change that.'

'I hear you.' Alexa gulped in a few deep breaths to steady her heartbeat. She did hear him and even though she might like to fix things for him that wasn't her role.

The following night Alexa smiled at Stevens as he opened her car door and waited for her to exit onto the damp London street.

An avant-garde restaurant loomed ahead, illuminated by a single bright light; the black door and grey brickwork looked as if it hid an illegal gin joint rather than a Michelin star restaurant.

Rafe's security team moved ahead of them, clearing the way and entering the building first.

Trying to lighten the mood between them that had shifted since she'd accepted Regan's invitation, Alexa chatted as if nothing was wrong.

'I've heard of this restaurant. The chef is some sort of food maestro. I read that he creates new recipes in a laboratory rather than a kitchen.'

'He's innovative,' Rafe agreed. 'And good at what he does.'

'Something you admire.'

'I admire lots of things.' His gaze slid down her body as the maître d' took her coat. 'Like you in that dress.'

Relieved that he no longer seemed upset with her, Alexa smiled. 'I believe you said that back at the apartment.'

'No, I nearly stripped it off you back in the apartment. Somehow I've convinced myself that anticipation will make the pleasure worth waiting for and didn't want to disappoint you by cancelling tonight.'

As usual the explosive chemistry that was never far below the surface when they were together ignited, stealing her breath.

'I'm glad you didn't cancel,' she murmured. 'I think it's going to be really special. And this dress deserved an outing because I'll never be able to wear it in Berenia.' Alexa adjusted the shoestring straps over her shoulders. The dress was low-cut at the front, even more daring than the one she'd worn to Bound, and it made her feel sexy and confident—exactly how Rafe always made her feel.

Buoyed by a mixture of renewed happiness and lust, Alexa glanced at him from beneath the sweep of her lashes. 'But I look forward to what anticipation looks like later on.'

'I can tell you what it will look like.' Rafe placed his hand against the small of her back and leant close. 'A tenth of a second.'

Alexa gave a husky laugh and suddenly she was plastered up against Rafe's hard body. She gasped at the unexpected contact and the doorman discreetly glanced at his feet.

'Stay an extra week,' he said gruffly.

'What?'

'Don't leave tomorrow. It's too soon. Stay an extra week. You can work from my place if you need to. I've hardly scratched the surface of what I want to show you.'

Dazed by the forceful nature of his request, Alexa's mind blanked of everything but him. She was sure there were a hundred good reasons why she should say no, not least because she wanted to stay with him in London a little *too* much, but she couldn't utter any of them. 'I'd love to.'

'Good.' A satisfied smile curved his lips just before they connected with hers for a brief searing kiss. 'Now let's go and get tonight over with.'

Giddy with delight that Rafe wanted to be with her as much as she wanted to be with him, Alexa floated through the sliding steel door into a large room that had once been an old warehouse. The designers had kept many of the original features, including industrial lighting suspended from black cables and exposed beams along the walls. Long tables dressed with pristine white tablecloths and sparkling silverware filled the space, with a brushed metal bar running along the back wall.

Most of the guests seemed to already be present, about forty people standing in small groups holding champagne flutes and chatting animatedly.

A waiter in a white coat stopped in front of them, holding a tray full of coloured drinks.

'Mimosas,' Rafe murmured, obviously reading her perplexed expression correctly. 'Chilled juice and champagne. You might like it.'

Alexa accepted the pink drink, her eyes wide with appreciation at the sweet taste. 'I do like it.'

Rafe's eyes gleamed, but he had no chance to respond as Regan carefully crossed the room to greet them. She looked amazing in a gold three-quarter-length dress that cleverly hid her massive baby bump.

'I don't know much about pregnant ladies,' Rafe said, bending to kiss his sister-in-law on the cheek, 'but you look ready to pop.'

'Rafe!' Alexa admonished. 'You don't say that to a pregnant woman. You look amazing, Your Majesty. I hope I look as beautiful as you when I'm eight months pregnant.'

'Thanks. But please call me Regan.' Her eyes sparkled with merriment, her hand cradling her stomach. 'I'm not due for a month yet, but the sooner this little darling comes out the better. I feel like a hippopotamus.'

'My thoughts exactly,' Rafe deadpanned.

'I'll make him pay later,' Alexa promised. 'Where's the birthday boy?' She held out a silver-wrapped gift Rafe had organised earlier in the day.

'I'll take that,' Regan offered. 'And Jag is with a good friend who is plying him with some sort of whisky that was created in a cave five hundred leagues below the sea, or some such. You should join them, Rafe, while I introduce Alexa to the other guests.'

'Love to.' Rafe gently touched Alexa's jaw. 'You okay with that, Princess?'

Alexa's heart bumped behind her chest at the

sweet endearment she'd come to love. 'Of course,' she said, watching as he walked away.

'Wow,' Milena said by way of a greeting as she stopped beside Alexa. 'I never thought I'd see the day my brother looked at a woman like that.' Quirky and exuberant in an orange dress and bright blue stockings, she grinned delightedly at Alexa. 'But it had to happen one day, right?'

Alexa knew she thought Rafe was in love with her, but that was because Milena had no idea that they'd married for political purposes. Alexa hated lying to her, but she knew that the less people who knew their relationship was staged the better.

'We're having a good time together,' Alexa supplied, which was true enough. They were having a very good time together. Or at least she was. She frowned a little as she gazed over at Rafe, greeting the men beside the bar. She was pretty sure Rafe was too. At least she knew he was in the bedroom. Just as the thought formed in her head, Rafe glanced back at her, his blue eyes finding hers with unerring accuracy.

'Can you both excuse me?' Regan said. 'I need to remind the caterers about the cake.'

'I'll take care of Alexa,' Milena promised, snagging a champagne flute from a passing waiter. 'You know my brother can't stop looking at you,' she mused happily. 'And whatever you've done to soften him, I'm glad.'

'Soften him?'

'Yeah, he actually listened to me the other day when I called him to complain about the amount of security Jag was insisting I have with me when I move to New York next week. He even promised to speak with him about it to see if he could reduce it.'

'He's worried you'll get taken advantage of. And there are a lot of toads out there,' Alexa said. 'Believe me, I know.'

'I suppose you're right,' Milena conceded. 'But I'm not thinking about that. I believe in destiny so whatever happens, happens. I'm just happy for my two brothers. One about to become a father, the other so in love he'd walk over hot coals for you. I still find it hard to believe, and I can't wait until you become Queen and Rafe has to walk two paces behind you at all times.' She gave Alexa an impish look. 'Given that he likes to always be in charge, I plan to tease him shamelessly about his subservient position every chance I get.'

Alexa knew that Milena meant well with her sisterly digs, but her comment struck a chord deep inside Alexa. In Berenia the spouses of a monarch didn't walk two paces behind; they walked ten paces behind.

And Rafe would never do it.

Moreover, she'd never ask him to do it.

And she'd like to be able to tell Milena that. Tell her that, actually, she didn't love Rafe at all. But even as the words formed in her mind she knew that not only could she not say them for reasons of confidentiality; but because they were no longer true.

She had gone and done the inconceivable and fallen in love with him, she realised with a sickening jolt. She didn't know when, or how, her feelings had changed, but she knew that they had, and the need to protect herself, to hide herself away from prying eyes threatened to overwhelm her.

She'd been so careful to keep their relationship in context. Tried so hard to remain objective and not to make more of their connection than was actually there, even embracing Rafe's ability to separate emotion and sex, and yet…at the end of the day she found him as utterly irresistible as most other women he'd dated. Because underneath that layer of sophistication and rebellious charm was a man who was caring and loyal and strong. A man who was worth keeping.

Her dream man.

Only she wasn't his dream woman. And she never would be because, although he clearly enjoyed spending time with her, he didn't want anything more from her. He didn't want that from any woman.

'Are you okay, Alexa?'

Milena placed a hand on her arm, her exotic eyes clouded with concern. 'You look a little dazed. Do you need to sit down? I hope it wasn't something I said. I know Rafe won't mind walking behind you. I should never have joked about that.'

Rafe was right, she thought with self-disgust; she really did need to work on her poker face if Milena had picked up on her distress so easily.

'I'm fine,' she automatically assured the other woman. 'I think this mimosa has gone to my head.'

'You need food,' Milena said. 'If I drink without eating I get lightheaded too. Let me find you some of the delicious canapés the waiters have been passing around.'

Alexa knew that an empty stomach was hardly enough to make her feel so dizzy. But realising she was in love with a man who would never love her back would do it.

She sucked in a deep breath. She was going to have to develop a new poker face and fast because this wasn't information she could ever reveal to Rafe. Everything would instantly change if she did. He'd see her as some lovesick fool like the women in his past who couldn't control their feelings for him. He might even withdraw from her like he had the day before, feel sorry for her, look at her with sympathy or, worse, worry that she would try to cling to him when it was time to end their marriage.

Right now she was his equal in and out of the bedroom. Right now they were having a good time, a wonderful time, but all she would have to do to ruin that would be to utter those three tiny little words and it would be gone. He'd probably send her home immediately, making up some excuse to avoid seeing her again. It would be awful.

And it was her fault. She'd become attached when she'd promised him that she wouldn't. When she'd promised *herself* that she wouldn't.

But she wasn't a dreamer in need of a fairy tale ending. She was a strong woman in charge of her own destiny.

Destiny.

There was that word again. And the irony of how her destiny had yet again interfered with her love life wasn't lost on her. Because even if Rafe did—by some miracle of the universe—have feelings for her it would never work out between them. While Stefano had wanted to marry her for who she was, Rafe *didn't* want to be married to her for who she was. He had made it clear on multiple occasions that he had no wish to return to Santara. That he hated all things to do with duty and royalty, so it stood to reason that he'd never want to move to Berenia. And while she could abdicate and pass the crown onto her cousin, it wasn't ideal because—

Abdicate?

Stumbling into a chair, Alexa threw her hands out to stop herself from falling when she was grabbed from behind and pulled up against a hard male body that sent tingles to her toes.

'Whoa.' Rafe reached for the half-empty champagne flute she'd nearly upended all over herself, grabbing it in time to prevent any of the pink contents from spilling. 'Careful, Princess.' He nuzzled her neck indulgently. 'You have a habit of spilling brightly coloured drinks all over yourself. At least this time you're not wearing white.'

Distracted by his lips against the tender skin of her neck, it took Alexa's dazed brain a moment to realise what he'd said. When it sank in she spun around in the circle of his arms and stared up at him.

'You?' Her gaze collided with his sparkling blue eyes as her brain rearranged the events of her past into a new world order. 'It was you. It was *always* you.'

Her heart lurched inside her chest and she didn't know whether to laugh or cry at the realisation that he had been the one to save her from embarrassment all those years ago, not his brother.

Her heart gripped tight inside her chest as she stared at his beautiful face. Him. It had always been him.

Destiny, whispered through her head again and she could have burst into tears on the spot. Because he wasn't her destiny at all. He wasn't her anything.

Bemused, Rafe cocked his head to the side as if he hadn't heard her right. 'Always me?'

'Yes.' How had she mistaken him for his brother all those years ago? How had she *not* known?

But then Rafe enjoyed playing the bad boy so much, how could she have ever thought that it would have been him? Who would have thought that the Rebel Prince would have possessed the empathy to prevent a young girl from embarrassing herself in front of a room full of dignitaries? But he'd always been that person deep down. It was why women fell over themselves to have a piece of him. Rafe was charming and debonair and handsome as the devil, but he possessed a deep sensitivity that eclipsed everything else. It was why his father's continual rejection had hurt him so much that the only way he'd been able to survive it was to pretend that it didn't hurt at all. It was why he reacted so strongly whenever he felt judged. He cared about those he loved, she realised, perhaps a little too much.

'Stop monopolising your new bride, Rafe,' Milena teased. 'She needs to eat!'

Feeling raw and exposed, Alexa gratefully accepted the small plate of canapés Milena offered. She knew her stomach wouldn't hold anything down, but at least nibbling at the food would give her enough time to develop an A-grade poker face.

Because she was going to need it to get through the rest of the night with her heart intact.

CHAPTER NINE

RAFE WATCHED ALEXA join his sister at the table, a slight frown pleating his brow. He would swear there was something up with her, but she wouldn't catch his eye so that he could be sure.

He'd taken her away this week on the spur of the moment and he'd enjoyed himself more than he'd thought possible. Being a loner, he usually couldn't wait to leave whoever he was with to get back to his own company, but that urge didn't seem to arise with Alexa.

He knew he liked her more than was wise, but he didn't seem to have any control over that. Looking at her, with her midnight-black hair catching the glints of the down lights and her perfect lips tilted into a smile, he wondered, not for the first time, at his total lack of control around this woman. Like asking her to stay an extra week because he didn't want her to leave.

She'd burrowed under his skin and although he was still waiting for the novelty factor to wear off, it wasn't happening. If anything, the more time he spent with her, the more he wanted to, which had never happened to him before.

Pleasure was pleasure but this… Being with her went beyond that and he'd be kidding himself if he tried to convince himself otherwise. He liked her both in and out of the bedroom. He liked her curiosity about the world, her dedication to her country, her loyalty to her people. He liked the way she teased him and challenged him and he loved that she shared his sense of adventure, and that she wanted to make the world a better place for everyone. Even him.

He'd been wrong to call her a doormat; she was far from a doormat. She was loyal and honourable and dedicated. They were all qualities he admired and tried to adhere to himself. He just wished her dedication was focused his way, rather than Berenia.

But then, if it was, what would he do with it? It wasn't as if he was looking for a permanent arrangement. They'd married with the express intention that it would end. She wanted it to end. And so did he.

Didn't he?

Well, of course he did. Alexa was as constrained by her royal duties as his brother was, giving her little choice as to how to live her life.

For a man committed to living his life with

as few encumbrances as possible that would never work.

'You still thinking of ending things with Alexa in six months' time?'

Rafe gave his brother a blank stare. Jag had always had the uncanny knack of knowing what he was thinking. The fact that he'd been staring at Alexa for a full five minutes might have also given him away. 'Of course.'

'Okay.'

Jag joined him in watching Alexa chatting with the other women who had joined her and their sister at the table, sipping his glass of red.

'Okay? That's it?' He cut his brother a brooding glance. 'You're not even going to try and tell me I'm wrong? Not going to try and give me some brotherly advice?'

A smile threatened to break out on Jag's face. 'Would you like me to give you some brotherly advice?'

'No.' Rafe didn't need advice. Especially about his love life. And since when did he think of sleeping with a woman as his 'love life'?

'You sure?' Jag asked. 'You look a little torn.'

Did he? Well, hell. 'I'm not torn. Alexa is… she's great. But she's not looking for anything long-term and nor am I. You know that.'

'I know some things are bigger than we are,' Jag answered enigmatically. 'But the Rebel

Prince and the future Queen of Berenia? It would never work, would it?'

'No, it wouldn't.' Rafe's expression turned grim. 'You know I can't toe the royal line if I don't agree with it.'

'That's always been one of your great strengths, Rafa. You speak your mind. Alexa would no doubt appreciate having someone like that in her corner when she starts her reign.'

'Father didn't.'

'No. But he was an ass.'

Rafe gave a short bark of laughter. 'Not to put too fine a point on it.'

Jag grinned, and suddenly it was as if they were teenagers again and racing each other across the sand in dune buggies.

'Remember that day in—'

'The mountains? Yeah. I beat you to the top that day.'

Jag scoffed. 'We'll call it even. But I definitely won the—'

'You wish,' Rafe cut in on a laugh. 'I've always been better than you at fencing.'

'Dream on, lover boy. I'll give you a rematch any time you're game. But I was talking about the yacht race around the sound.'

'A close call, I admit. But again, lucky.'

Jag laughed at the outrageous call. He'd always

been the better yachtsman, while Rafe had excelled at dune racing.

He'd been wrong to dread tonight, Rafe realised with a jolt of clarity. Wrong to put so much distance between him and Jag over his guilty conscience because he had missed his brother. Missed his easy companionship.

'Listen, Jag…' he let out a slow breath '… I need to apologise for walking away all those years ago when you became King. I should have stayed to help with the transition.'

Jag gave him a look. 'There's nothing to apologise for. I wanted you to go. You'd lived under Father's iron rule for far too long. Staying would have stifled you even more.'

'Still—'

'It's okay, Rafa. We're—'

Whatever Jag had been about to say was cut off when his eyes turned as hard as stone. Seconds later he was striding across the room to where Regan leant against the back of a chair, one hand cradling her belly.

Noticing nothing out of place, Rafe followed, wondering at the tense set of his brother's shoulders.

'Goddamn it, Regan, I knew we shouldn't have come here tonight,' Jag said, steel lining every word, his hard gaze riveted to his wife.

'Don't swear,' Regan admonished. 'I got the all-clear to fly this weekend, remember?'

Sick with dread that his brother's seemingly solid relationship had gone the way of his parents', Rafe was about to step between them, as he had done with his parents many times during his youth, when Regan let out a low moan. 'How was I to know that my waters would break tonight?'

Her waters had broken?

Comprehension dawned on Rafe in a brutal rush.

'If something happens to you,' Jag ground out, his voice ragged with emotion, 'I'll never forgive myself.'

'Nothing will happen. I'm in labour. I'm not dying.'

'A month early!'

'Babies come early all the time. It's——' Her breath cut off as another contraction hit her. Jag swore and lifted her into his arms.

Acting purely on instinct, Rafe pulled his phone from his pocket, dialling the emergency services as his eyes searched for Alexa.

Before he'd located her, he felt her hand go into his, squeezing gently. 'What can I do?'

'What you are doing.' He brought her fingers to his lips, his worried eyes on his sister-in-law and brother. After organising emergency services he dialled another number, relieved when the call was answered on the first ring.

A ripple went through the room as the guests started to get wind of what was happening.

'The ambulance is two minutes away,' Rafe told his brother. 'And a friend of mine who is probably the best obstetrician in Britain will meet us at the emergency door of the hospital.'

'Thanks.' Jag swallowed hard, his eyes watering.

'She's going to be fine,' Rafe assured him. 'You focus on her. I'll take care of everything else.'

Two hours later, Rafe felt ragged as he waited for news, any news, that Regan was okay and the baby had been delivered safe and well. He'd never felt so helpless as he had at the sight of his powerful brother brought to his knees with worry.

This was why he wanted nothing to do with love. It churned you up inside and spat you out, battered, at the other end. It was such a stupid emotion. He had no idea why people actually sought this kind of thing out.

As if reading his thoughts, Alexa glanced at him from across the room. Two steps and she'd be in his arms and he'd feel one hundred times better, but he resisted the urge. He didn't want that. He didn't want to rely on someone else to make him happy.

But wasn't that already what had happened? All week he'd talked with her, laughed with her, held her in his arms and danced with her and that was exactly how he'd felt. Happy. Content. *Complete.*

Two of Chase's top security operatives stood to attention at the door of the waiting room, four more coordinating with Jag's special envoy outside the building and outside the delivery suite.

'I'm sure she's fine,' Alexa offered tentatively, a wary expression clouding her eyes. She was only trying to make him feel better so why wasn't he holding her? Comforting her? Taking comfort *from* her?

'Coffee.' Milena returned, bearing three steaming mugs. 'The café is closed at this time, so it's vending machine only, I'm afraid, but what can you do?'

'Alexa doesn't drink coffee at night,' he said absently.

'I will tonight,' she said, straightening to go to his sister. 'I think I'd drink anything right now. Thanks for thinking of it.'

'I needed to do something and since Sherlock here—' Milena gestured to the Chase security expert Rafe had asked to stay with her during the whole proceedings '—wouldn't let me go for a walk, or go find a decent café, that's it.'

The security operative's expression didn't change as he handed over a bag of snacks to Milena.

She took it begrudgingly. 'And snacks. Anyone want one?'

Remembering how much fun he'd had feeding Alexa chocolates they'd bought that day at the market, his eyes cut to hers. As if her mind had deviated down the same path, her eyes turned smoky.

Breathing hard, he deliberately turned to his sister before he pulled Alexa into an unlocked supply closet and rid himself of all this tension with something stronger than coffee.

When he glanced back, Alexa had her bottom lip between her teeth and was staring at the floor. Before he could go to her a nurse pushed through the glass door.

Rafe's heart rose to his mouth.

The nurse smiled. 'It's a girl,' she said. 'And mother and baby are both healthy and doing well.'

A noisy breath shuddered out of his lungs. His sister whooped with joy and Alexa had a hand on her heart.

'Can we see them?'

'Of course. Her Majesty asked for all of you to come through.'

Almost dazed at the notion that he was an uncle, Rafe followed his sister and wife into the delivery suite.

The room was quiet as they entered, Regan reclining in the bed while Jag held a small bundle wrapped in white. For a woman who had just given birth, Regan looked awfully good. Not that Rafe had ever seen a woman straight after giving birth before.

'Oh, my… She's adorable,' Milena cooed. 'Congratulations.'

Grinning from ear to ear, Jag handed the precious bundle to his sister.

'I'm so grateful, Rafe,' Regan said, her brown eyes tired but filled with joy. 'Your brother completely lost it in my hour of need. If you hadn't stepped up I probably would have given birth on the dessert trolley.'

Jag scoffed at the very idea and Rafe turned away from the loved-up couple—only to freeze when he saw Alexa.

At some point Milena had passed the newborn over to her and she had his niece cradled against her chest, an adoring expression on her face.

A tight fist wrapped around his heart and squeezed. For a moment he couldn't breathe. Her long hair had drifted over one shoulder, glossy and black, her face a mask of serenity. It was like the time he'd first set eyes on her, another bolt of lightning hitting him square between the eyes, followed quickly by the sure knowledge that he could look at this woman for the rest of his life and never grow tired of it.

'Do you want to hold her?'

Somehow, Alexa was in front of him. Rafe frowned. *For the rest of his life?*

He saw her eyes widen. 'You've gone pale. If you don't want to…'

'No.' He kept his gaze on the baby in her arms. 'I'll hold her.'

As if he was standing on the outside looking in, he took the baby and cradled her in his arms. She was so tiny. So dainty. This perfect little being that was both vulnerable and needy. Taking in the glow on both her parents' faces, he knew that she would always be loved. She'd never have cause to feel insecure or abandoned by those she needed the most.

What would it be like if this was his child? His and Alexa's?

Emotion, thick and unwelcome, clogged his throat. Those feelings he'd had for her earlier increased tenfold. Feelings he'd never had for a woman before. Previously, his life had always seemed so clear-cut. One thing had led on to another and he'd never questioned it. He'd just gone with it and cared little about the outcome. But he cared now, he realised. He cared very much.

* * *

Alexa had never felt more like running than she did right now. When she had passed the baby to Rafe all she'd thought about was how it would feel if that tiny angel belonged to both of them. The chilly expression on his face told her that he most definitely had not been thinking the same thing.

As a result the car ride back to the apartment had been quiet, as if they were both lost in their own thoughts. But it wasn't a happy quiet as it should have been after the safe arrival of a baby. It was fraught with unspoken emotions. It was as if all the closeness of the past week had fallen away as if it had never existed. And perhaps it hadn't outside her own imagination.

As soon as they arrived at the apartment Alexa didn't wait around to see what Rafe intended to do; instead she headed for the spare room she'd been allocated and pulled her suitcase out of the walk-in wardrobe.

'What are you doing?'

Heart thumping, Alexa turned and blinked at him. His eyes were unreadable as he took in her suitcase and the clothing in her hands.

'Packing.'

'It's nearly midnight.'

'I know.' She flashed him a bright smile. 'Your odd hours must have rubbed off on me.'

Intensely aware of him watching her, she kept

her movements smooth and unruffled as she folded a shirt and placed it in the case.

'I thought you were staying an extra week.'

'I was but then I remembered that I have a number of meetings booked in for Monday that I can't miss.' She knew she was rambling but she couldn't seem to take a breath deep enough to oxygenate her brain.

'Get your father to attend them.'

'I can't. I'm sorry. I didn't think it through enough when you asked me to stay earlier. How beautiful is your niece, though? I love the name, Jana. It really suits her.'

'Forget the baby,' he growled. 'And leave the damn clothes where they are.' His hands descended on her shoulders as he turned her to face him, his jaw tight. 'I need you, Alexa. I need to touch you. I need to make love to you.'

There was something in his eyes Alexa had never seen before. A depth of emotion she knew had come from experiencing anxiety about the unexpected birth of his niece. It had affected her too, making her want to find space so she could process everything. But she could no more deny Rafe than she could stop the cycles of the moon.

Gazing up at him, she let her eyes drift over the hard planes of his face. This was what happened, she reminded herself brokenly, when you opened yourself up to uncertainty. You got hurt.

Because she had to go. She had to return to Berenia and pick up the reins of her normal life. She had to get back to what she knew, not only because it was what they had agreed upon from the start, but because she would only be staying an extra week in the vain hope that Rafe's feelings for her would change.

And she wouldn't torture herself like that. Not a second time. And not with a man who already had too much of her heart, little did he know it.

'Stay.' He cupped her face in his hands.

Alexa's heart felt as if it had just cleaved in two at the look in his eyes, the anguish of her own emotions like a chokehold around her throat. She so desperately wanted to tell him how she felt, tell him that if he needed her she'd be his for ever, but fortunately he kissed her and she stopped thinking altogether. Stopped trying to make this into something that it wasn't and gave into the passion between them, winding her arms around his neck and holding him tight for the last time.

When he woke in the morning Rafe knew she was gone. There was an emptiness in the room, a silence in his apartment he hadn't felt since before she had arrived.

An icy feeling of disappointment entered his heart, followed by a hot rush of anger. Of course she had left like this. Stealing away in the middle of the night as if she'd never even been here. He'd known she'd wanted to go, and yet he'd asked her to stay anyway. No, *begged* her to stay. A futile exercise.

Thrusting back the covers, he pulled on his clothes and headed for the kitchen. She'd left a note. A pitiful piece of paper that thanked him for a wonderful week, asking him to call her if he needed her for anything.

As if he'd do that.

He might have had feelings for her last night, feelings that ran deeper than any he'd ever experienced before with any other woman, but that had only been because of the drama surrounding the birth of his niece. It had unlocked something inside him—some emotion that had made him think, for the barest second, that he was in fact in love with Alexa.

Thank God he hadn't told her that during the heat of their lovemaking during the night. Thank God he hadn't confused sex with emotion when that was all it had ever been.

Intense, yes. Controlling at times. But love… no. This wasn't love. This was white-hot fury that he'd allowed a woman to get under his skin and she'd walked out on him in the middle of the night.

Had she thought he couldn't handle seeing her leave? That he'd try and stop her?

He wouldn't have. Not a second time.

CHAPTER TEN

RAFE GLARED AT the pile of paperwork on his desk as if the fierceness of his stare might get it done without him having to actually do anything. The promise of spring had completely left London, and rain lashed the windows of his office as if some angry god were throwing spears from the sky.

Not that he cared. He wasn't planning to leave any time soon and when he did he'd just be going home to an empty apartment.

Still, the gloom of the exterior seemed to invade the office, casting a dim glow that not even the bright lights inside could drive away.

Another email pinged into his inbox just as Hannah knocked on his door. Knowing that his EA would be harder to ignore, he turned towards the door, his jaw clenching when instead of Hannah standing in his doorway it was Milena in a bright pink coat, her hair cut into an edgy long bob.

He'd successfully dodged his family prior to

Jag flying Regan and his precious daughter, Princess Jana, home by explaining that he was coming down with something and hadn't wanted to infect the baby. Which had been true. He'd felt like death warmed up for the past eight days. But now his sister had caught up with him.

'I thought you had left for New York,' he said pleasantly, deciding that heading her off at the pass was his best game opener.

'I had some things to finish up in Oxford before I left.' She strolled closer and flopped down in the chair opposite his desk. 'Then Hannah staged an intervention so here I am.'

Rafe frowned. 'Hannah did what?'

'Staged an intervention.' Milena's eyes moved over his face with deliberate slowness. 'I have to confess I can see why she did. You look awful.'

'I haven't shaved for—' he couldn't remember '—a few days. That hardly constitutes awful.'

'You haven't slept for a few days either, if the circles beneath your eyes are anything to go by.'

'Forgot to moisturise.'

'Ha! What's up?' Her voice went soft, her gaze following suit. Rafe ground his teeth together.

'Work,' he intoned. 'Now, is there any other reason for your visit?'

'How's Alexa?'

She reached for the glass paperweight on his desk and started fiddling with it.

His eyes narrowed at her innocuous tone. 'Is this one of your trick questions?'

He hadn't spoken to Alexa since she'd walked out of his life and he couldn't be sure if Milena knew that or not.

'No, this is me trying to ease into the conversation without getting my head bitten off.' She gave a sigh. 'I know Alexa is back in Berenia. Jag told me.'

'Did he also tell you why?'

'He told me that your marriage wasn't all that it seemed, if that's what you mean.'

Rafe gave a harsh bark of laughter. 'Always the diplomat, our brother.' He ran a hand through his hair. 'Look, he's right. Alexa and I married for political reasons and, according to recent reports, it seems to be working. I'm considering it my good deed for Santara.'

'Sorry, I'm not buying it,' Milena said bluntly. 'I know you, Rafe. You didn't just marry her for political reasons. It was real. I was there. I saw you both say your vows to each other. I saw you kiss her at the altar.'

The last thing he wanted was to remember kissing Alexa and he turned back to his computer. 'It's done, Milena. In three thousand, four hundred and thirty-two hours we'll be divorced.'

'Oh, Rafe.'

Pushing out of his chair in frustration, Rafe

glared at his sympathetic sister before stalking to the window. He angled himself against the window, wishing he was standing out there so that the icy blasts could numb the sudden pain in his chest.

'You really, really love her, don't you?' Milena prodded gently.

'If this is love you can have it,' he growled. 'Next time I accuse you of the same thing you can throw this back in my face.'

'I don't want to throw this back in your face. I want to help you fix it. But I think you're afraid.'

'Really?' He didn't try to keep the sneer from his voice. 'First Alexa, and now you. What exactly do you think I'm afraid of?'

'Feeling. Love.'

Rafe scoffed. 'Love doesn't exist.' Even if for a brief moment he had thought he'd felt it for Alexa. 'And if you go around thinking it does you'll experience a world of pain.'

'Like we did as kids? I was young when Mum left but I remember how upset you were. You punched a hole in the wall, remember? You broke two knuckles and had to have your hand bandaged for six weeks.'

'How do you know I punched the wall?'

'I saw you. And ever since then, it seems to me, you've closed your heart off to everyone around you. Including me and Jag.'

Rafe gave her a bleak look. 'I'm always there for you if you need me, you know that.'

'I do.' She touched his arm. 'But you won't let us be there for you when you need us.'

'That's because I don't need anyone.'

But the words rang hollow inside his heart. If he didn't need anyone why didn't he feel okay with Alexa leaving? Why did his life seem so colourless all of a sudden?

Rafe swore.

Milena smiled. 'I know love isn't a comfortable concept for you but she loves you too.'

'How would you know?'

'The same way I know you love her. It's the way you look at each other. Like the other person is the most perfect person in the world for you. Jag and Regan have the same thing going on, and I swear one day I want someone to look at me the way you two look at your wives.'

Fear made him want to snap at her and say it wasn't true but, unfortunately, what she said fitted. It explained the hard lump in his throat on the morning he'd woken to find Alexa gone, and the hollow feeling inside him every day since. It explained why for the first time in his adult life he didn't want to get out of bed in the morning and face the day.

Rafe let his head fall into his hands and acknowledged what he'd always known to be true.

He loved his wife. He loved Alexa, and it wasn't going to go away.

He remembered noticing her at a formal function when she had been a shy teenager on the verge of womanhood. Even then there had been something compelling about her that had held his attention. Something about her that had made him want to protect her.

But her loving him in return?

'I think you're forgetting that she left, Milena. If you love someone you don't walk out on them in the middle of the night.'

'Like our mother?' she asked softly. 'Alexa isn't our mother, Rafe. And who knows what would have happened if our father had gone after her? Maybe she would have come back and our life would have turned out very differently.'

'I don't know—'

'And you won't if you give up.'

Those words jolted something deep inside him. 'I don't give up.'

His sister's brow arched. 'So why haven't you asked her why she left instead of presuming that you already know the answer?'

Because he was petrified of stuffing things up and feeling like a fool. Because he was petrified of feeling even worse than he did now. If that was even possible.

'How did you get to be so smart?'

'Observing two thick-headed brothers my whole life.'

Rafe gave her a faint smile and palmed his keys. 'I owe you one,' he said, heading for the door.

'I know.' She grinned broadly. 'And I'll be sure to collect on it.'

Alexa flicked through the pages of notes Nasrin had printed out for her. She was up to page twenty of fifty so she really needed to get a wriggle on if she was going to at least know something of the details about the one hundred guests who would be attending tonight's trade dinner. Usually she would have done this already, but she couldn't seem to muster the enthusiasm for it right now.

She knew what was wrong. She'd been back in Berenia for just over a week and nothing felt right. Not that anyone would guess. She'd upped her game face and had been putting on a good front. Had been trying to convince herself that it was silly to feel bad about something that had only been temporary to begin with. Which was exactly what she'd said to Nasrin when she'd been confronted with her EA's crestfallen face.

'But I was sure it was going to work out,' Nasrin had moaned when she'd returned *sans* Rafe.

'The way you looked at each other at the wedding. *That* kiss.'

The way Alexa remembered it, Rafe had been horrified to see her walk down the aisle, and she'd been similarly placed—or rather displaced—so she had no idea what Nasrin was talking about.

It had taken half an hour of convincing, but finally Nasrin had gone quiet on the subject, or perhaps she'd gone quiet because she'd had no choice. Either way, Alexa had been relieved to not have to talk about Rafe.

Her father had naturally asked where her husband was and when he planned to move to Berenia, but Alexa had put him off too, turning the topic of the conversation to business to distract him, all the while knowing that she really needed to come clean about her marriage sooner rather than later.

And she would. She'd just needed another week or so to mourn in private before she closed the 'Rafe' chapter of her life. She supposed it had been cowardly to sneak out of his apartment while he'd been asleep, but at the time she hadn't cared. She'd just wanted it to be easy. And she'd left him a note. *Thanks for everything. Call if you need me.*

Of course he hadn't called; she hadn't expected that he would. And that was okay, because that was easier too.

'Are you ready, Your Highness?'

Alexa glanced at Nasrin and gave a silent groan. She was still on page twenty, the illness she'd been fighting since her return to Berenia making her feel dizzy at times. 'I haven't quite finished the notes you made. Is there anything in particular I should be aware of? Any topics of conversation I need to avoid?'

Nasrin rattled off a couple of things for her to consider but Alexa had to force herself to concentrate. Don't mention climate change to the Minister of the Russian Interior, and remember to congratulate the Ambassador of France on their latest election results, and absolutely steer clear of the Prince of Tongase because he would bend her ear back about export deals given half a chance.

Logging the details in her memory, Alexa gave her reflection a quick once-over. She'd opted for a simple navy blue sheath tonight and pinned her hair back into a tightly coiled bun.

Her image said that she meant business and she did. The time she'd spent with Rafe lazing around in bed or exploring the countryside was like a distant dream that had happened to someone else.

'The King and Queen of Santara sent a thank you card for Princess Jana's gift. They won't be attending tonight, but that was to be expected.

The King hasn't left his wife's side since the birth.'

Alexa gave Nasrin a small smile. The last thing she wanted to hear about was how much the King of Santara cared about his Queen. 'And my father?'

'He's waiting for you in the south parlour. Are you sure you're up to this, Your Highness? You look a little pale.'

'I'm fine.'

She wasn't fine. She wanted to lie down in her bed and go to sleep. Maybe for one hundred years. Smiling at the irony of how her mind had turned to a fairy tale, she shook her head. She'd been awakened by her very own Prince Charming—literally—but he still hadn't wanted her in the end. He hadn't even attempted to contact her since she'd left. Not that she'd wanted him to. A clean break was much better.

Heading to the south parlour, she knocked quietly before entering and found her father leaning against the fireplace. His eyes scanned her and he scowled. 'You don't look well.'

Alexa grimaced. 'Thank you, Father. The same goes for you.' Her father had been fighting a head cold since she'd returned, probably what she was struggling with herself, and should have been in bed. 'I'm more than happy to attend tonight's dinner without you if you'd rather rest.'

'I can rest when I'm dead,' her father argued. 'And you should have support tonight. That husband of yours should be here.'

Alexa had been hoping he wouldn't bring up Rafe's absence again but...so be it.

She gave a faint smile at the memory of the last time Rafe had muttered those words. Sealing his fate in agreeing to marry her.

But she couldn't think about Rafe right now, not in that way; she'd probably start leaking tears all over the place and her father would guess how devastated she was. But maybe now was the time to mention the true nature of her relationship with Rafe. That way, her father wouldn't have a lot of time to grill her about it, and it would give him time to process the details before they met up next.

Taking the bull by the horns, Alexa perched on the chair opposite the fireplace. 'Before we head down the stairs there's something I need to tell you about Prince Rafaele and myself. And I want you to know from the outset that the whole idea was mine so any complaints or issues you have should be solely directed at me.'

To give him his due, her father listened patiently as she gave him the CliffsNotes version as to what had happened, leaving out the part where she had fallen hopelessly in love with her husband and how he didn't love her back. That he would never love her back. Her father didn't need to know everything.

But she told him the rest. She told him about her proposal, and Rafe turning her down; she told him how they had never meant to actually go through with the wedding, and the marriage bargain they'd worked out between them. She also told him that Rafe had turned out to be nothing like she'd expected, and that he was actually a decent, hard-working man who cared deeply about those he loved. 'And now I'm back,' she said, struggling to remain composed. 'And, as you can see, ready to resume my duties.'

'I see. So what happens now?' he asked, his frown revealing how unimpressed he was with her actions.

'Now we stay married for five more months, and then quietly go our separate ways.'

'You should have told me this earlier.'

'Would you have listened?'

Previously, Alexa would never have asked her father such an impertinent question, but he needed to know that she wasn't the same person she had been before she'd married Rafe. She'd grown up in Rafe's arms and she didn't want to go back to the way things had been before. With her ostensibly being a yes person to please her father.

'Perhaps not,' he conceded. 'But I'm listening now.' He straightened his cuffs. 'However, it is time we went down to the receiving line. Our guests will be arriving at any moment.

'Of course. But Father…' Alexa mulled over her next words. 'I know you don't feel that I'm able to do this job alone, but I'm going to prove you wrong. I will make a worthy Queen of Berenia in Sol's stead.'

Her father stopped and frowned at her. 'I've never thought you incapable of being anything but an incredible leader of our people. But this is a lonely job, Alexa. It will be harder for you to find a suitable spouse once you become Queen, and I don't want you to rule alone. It's too hard.'

Her father's lined face turned weary and Alexa's heart jumped in alarm. 'Father—'

'I'm fine. Just… I miss your mother. And never more so than when you are opposite me looking as beautiful as she once was.'

'But I never knew that was how you felt.'

A faint smile twisted her father's lips. 'Why do you think I never remarried? There was no one to replace her. And I didn't want that for you. Rightly or wrongly, I didn't want you or Sol to become so attached to anyone that losing them would make you feel this empty.'

'Hence the reason you changed our nannies and tutors so often,' she said, finally understanding the logic behind that decision.

'I wanted you both to become more resilient than I felt at the time. Stronger. But you were hurt by love anyway, and then we lost Sol. I felt like I had failed you both.'

'Father—'

'Let me finish.' He grimaced as if explaining such deeply emotional issues was akin to having his skin flayed from his body. 'I thought that if I could force you to make a practical match it would save you from unnecessary heartache in the future. I can see that I was gravely mistaken about that. But finding you a life match was never about your capability to do your job. I hope you believe that.'

Alexa's stomach clenched tight. 'I don't know what to say.'

'There is nothing to say. You should have a strong man by your side to support you. And I hoped that Prince Rafaele would be that man.'

So had she. Or at least she had come to think that way. But while he was a very strong and compassionate man, he wasn't *her* strong and compassionate man. He might never be anyone's, given his need for independence and freedom from obligation.

Which was all she knew. Obligation and duty. Would those dual requirements always have to take precedence over love?

A lump lodged in her throat, threatening to

defeat her composure once more, and once more she pushed it back. 'Shall we go?'

'Yes. It is time.'

Three hours later Alexa knew that if she didn't sit down very soon she would likely fall down.

The head cold she'd been fighting made it hard to focus on the group currently discussing the merits of trade taxes and border control.

Offering to email one of their party some of the ideas her team had come up with on tax reform, Alexa made her excuses and was considering going to find a dark room to hole up in when her eyes snagged on a figure in black at the entrance to the ballroom.

Unable to believe that it was really Rafe, the hairs on the back of her neck rose when his eyes found her.

His expression was grim, his clothes as beautifully cut as they had been the night at the Children's Charity ball. But there was a wildness to him, and she realised that he hadn't shaved, giving him an even more dangerous edge than usual.

The guests he would have bowled over if they hadn't moved out of his way thought so too, their curious glances turning to wary alertness as they quickly moved out of his way.

Alexa only noticed them peripherally, her whole being focused entirely on Rafe.

He stopped directly in front of her, his frown darkening. 'Your hair is up.'

'Yes.' A wave of dizziness at having him standing in front of her made her instinctively reach out for him.

Rafe swore under his breath, taking hold of her elbow. 'And you're unwell.'

Shaking off her initial shock, Alexa cleared her throat, easing her arm out of his hold. 'Just a head cold. But you look…' Gorgeous. Commanding. And so desirable she wanted to throw herself into his arms and never let go. It seemed so unfair when she felt like death warmed up. 'Almost like your usual self.'

'I haven't been my usual self since we met, Princess,' he answered cryptically. 'That aside, I'm taking you out of here.'

Seriously rattled to have him here, Alexa shook her head. 'I can't leave yet. The speeches haven't happened.'

'Are you giving a speech?'

'No.'

'Then you're leaving.'

Alexa frowned. 'Rafe, you can't just turn up here and—'

'Prince Rafaele? So good of you to join us.'

Feeling a horrible sense of *déjà vu*, Alexa nearly groaned at the sound of her father's combative voice behind her, sure that he wouldn't back down now that he knew the truth of their marriage.

'You might not think that in a minute, Your Majesty,' Rafe answered. 'My wife is sick, and I'm taking her out of here.'

'Really?' King Ronan raised a brow. 'You've remembered that you have a wife, then?'

'I never forgot.' Rafe held her father's stare. 'Not even for a minute.'

Unable to decipher the silent code going on between the two men she was surprised to see her father nod his assent. 'Good. I told her she was not well. She needs to lie down.'

'I can make my own decisions,' Alexa said hotly, her voice low so as not to cause a scene.

'You can,' Rafe agreed. 'But we need to talk and I'd rather not do it in a room full of interested people.'

Suddenly aware that they were on the receiving end of about one hundred pairs of eyes, Alexa groaned. 'Okay, fine.'

Holding her head high, she started forward, her legs so shaky that she might have tripped over her skirts if Rafe hadn't caught her up in his arms without breaking stride.

'Put me down,' she urged. 'You're causing a scene.'

'Probably.' He gave her one of his devil-may-care grins. 'It is something I excel at, it seems.'

Alexa caught the surprised glance of the footman who scrambled to open a side door for them and just managed to resist burying her face against Rafe's neck.

'Which way are your rooms?' he asked gruffly.

'I'm not going to my room with you,' she said, knowing that if she did she really might throw herself at him. 'And I need you to put me down.'

Obliging her this time, he lowered her to the carpeted floor in one of the side rooms off the ballroom.

'Thank you.' She smoothed her hands down her dress, aware that she was in danger of placing meaning on his actions that probably didn't exist. 'What I need is to know what you're doing here. And why you look like you haven't had any sleep in a week.' Because this close, she could see that his eyes were not as bright as they usually were.

He grimaced. 'You and Milena should form a club. She thinks I look terrible as well.'

'I didn't say you looked terrible…but…why are you here, Rafe? What do you want?'

'Are you so desperate to get rid of me?' he asked softly.

No. She wasn't desperate to get rid of him. On the contrary she wanted him to stay. She wanted—

'Actually you have Milena to thank for my presence here tonight.'

'Oh.' A shaft of disappointment speared into her chest, bursting the little bubble of hope she'd been nursing that he'd come to Berenia for her. 'I'm not sure I understand. Does she need something from me?'

'No, Princess.' Rafe gave her a faint smile, his eyes so dark they were almost black. 'Milena doesn't want anything from you. She came to my office today and pointed out that I'm an idiot.'

'Rafe, I'm sure she didn't mean—'

'She did.' He took her face between his hands. 'Because she knows that I'm totally and utterly in love with you.'

Oh, God...

Alexa groaned softly. She knew Milena would have meant well, but she really wished the other woman hadn't interfered. 'I'm sorry she said that.' She shook her head, her hands trembling. 'She mentioned the same thing to me at Jag's party but I knew not to believe her. I knew—'

'You should have believed her.' Rafe placed a finger against her lips. 'Because she's right. I do love you.'

Alexa's eyes flew to his. 'How is that possible? At the hospital, when I handed you Princess Jana, you looked at me as if you never wanted to see me again.'

'That was shock. When I saw you holding the

baby all I could think about was how it would feel if Jana had been ours.'

'You did?' Her eyes turned watery because she felt so *emotional* hearing him say that. 'But you said you don't need love in your life.'

'I *didn't* want love in my life,' he corrected. 'Which is why I didn't go after you when you left. It was easier to let you go than to face how much I had come to need you. Especially since my mother left in the middle of the night and I woke the next morning to find her gone.'

'Oh, Rafe, I'm so sorry I reminded you of that. I didn't know what else to do. I was so afraid I'd blurt out how I felt and that you'd... It was cowardly.'

'I didn't exactly give you a lot of reasons to stay. I am now.' His hand smoothed over her jaw, tilting her face up to his. 'Tell me what you didn't want to blurt out last night.'

Alexa's smile was tremulous. 'That I love you, of course. That I think I've always loved you.'

Rafe crushed her lips beneath his, and for a moment all Alexa could do was cling to him. Then reality intruded with a thud.

'Rafe, wait...' Her voice shook and her knees threatened to give out as she eased back. 'This can't work. You know it can't. Your life is in London and I'm the future Queen, and unless I abdicate to my cousin I—'

'Abdicate?' Rafe took her face between his hands. 'Princess, nobody's abdicating. You're perfect for this role.'

'Then what are you suggesting? That we have a long-distance marriage?'

'Alexa, you're my wife. You're going to stay my wife, and I'm going to be your husband and support you in any way that I can. In Berenia.'

'You'll move to Berenia?'

He gave her a wide smile. 'What can I say? I'm a glutton for punishment. But my life is no longer in London. It's wherever you are.'

'But your business, your clubs…'

'I can run my business from anywhere if I choose to but seriously, Alexa, you're not hearing me. If you want it, my life is with you and wherever you are.'

'If I want it?'

'Yes. Do you? Do you want to spend the rest of your life with me as much as I want to spend the rest of mine with you?'

'Yes.' Finally giving into the insane level of happiness welling up inside her, Alexa laughed. 'Yes, yes, yes.'

She let out a shriek as Rafe wrapped his arms around her and swung her into the air. 'Rafe, I love you so much it scares me.'

'Only because you haven't come to trust how I feel yet. But you will. I plan to tell you every day so that you'll never feel insecure about your self-worth ever again.'

'I can't quite believe this,' she said, holding him tight. 'You were supposed to be the most unsuitable man on the planet.'

Rafe eased back so that he could look down into her face. 'And now?'

'Now I never want to let you go.' Giddy with emotion, she reached up onto her toes to kiss him and then pulled back at the last minute. 'We shouldn't. You'll catch my cold.'

'Princess, I don't think you have a cold. Your nose isn't even red.'

'My nose doesn't have to be red to have a cold. But I am sick. I feel dizzy sometimes and my stomach is unsettled a lot.'

'Have you seen a doctor?'

'No.'

'Then you should because I don't think you're ill. I think you're pregnant.'

'No, I'm not. I…' Alexa's eyes widened incredulously; her mind swung back to when her last period was due. She was late but in her misery she hadn't even noticed. 'I can't be.'

'There were a couple of times I didn't put a condom on right away.'

Alexa stared at him wide-eyed. 'Oh, God.' She clapped her hand over her mouth. 'What will we do?'

Rafe gave her a half smile. 'We'll have a baby.'

'I mean, will you mind if it's true?'

'Absolutely not,' he said huskily. 'I need to catch up to Jag, but…' His eyes grew wary. 'Do *you* want a baby?'

Knowing by the tense set of his shoulders that he was no doubt remembering his own childhood, Alexa clasped his face in her hands. 'If we have made a baby together I'll be the happiest woman in the world. I love you. I want to have your babies, and I intend to smother them in love and attention for ever.'

Rafe gave her a slow grin. 'Then how about you take me your room now, just in case I'm wrong. We can get to work immediately.'

Alexa threw her arms around his neck. 'With pleasure.'

EPILOGUE

RAFE HADN'T BEEN WRONG. Exactly two hundred
and seventy days after their wedding Zane and
Tobias had been born. Now they were rambunc-
tious one-year-olds.

'Milena, can you grab Jana and Zane before one
or both of them climb into the fountain again?'
Rafe asked, scooping his remaining twin up and
tucking him under his arm in a football hold before
he could think about joining his brother and cousin.

'On it!' Milena yelled, pretending to be a
wicked witch as she ran after the two children,
making them squeal with delight.

Seeing the fun his twin and older cousin were
having, Tobias let rip a loud squeal of indignation.

'Looks like you have your hands full!' Jag
laughed, burping one of his own newborn twins
against his shoulder. 'Where's Alexa?'

'Grabbing a coffee with Nasrin while she
checks in with her father. Okay, buddy.' Rafe
swung Tobias to the ground and waited for his
little legs to steady beneath him. 'Go pull some

more of Aunty Milena's hair out. We don't like the colour right now anyway.'

Tobias let out a war whoop and took off as fast as his legs would carry him. Rafe gave a loud sigh of relief. 'This parenting gig is harder than tending to a room full of Berenians with a chip on their shoulder.'

'Well, he is half Berenian,' Jag observed, patting his daughter's back.

Rafe gave him a bemused glance. 'Lucky for you that they are. Thanks to me, everything has completely settled down between our nations now. The Berenians love me.'

'Yeah, right.' His brother grinned back. 'And, speaking of Berenia, how's the new business venture?'

'Great. The new university is so popular we have to build more student accommodation to cope with demand.'

'You don't miss the nightclub scene?'

Since moving to Berenia, Rafe had sold off most of his clubs, keeping a few that Hannah had stepped into running for him. He now worked on restoring old buildings and returning them to their former glory and loved it.

He'd also opened up to his sister and brother, forging a bond with them that was deeper than ever.

'Everything is great,' he said, and meaning it.

'And you wouldn't swap it, right?'

Knowing Jag shared his sentiments, Rafe shook his head. 'Not in a heartbeat.'

'Where are the twins?'

His wife's voice from behind had Rafe swinging around. 'Princess.' Immediately at ease with her by his side, Rafe drew her into his arms and kissed her. 'The twins are over by the fountain with Milena. How's your father?'

'Determined to reign until he's ninety.'

Rafe laughed, kissing her again. 'I'm okay with that. The more time I get you all to myself the happier I am.'

'You'll always have me to yourself,' she promised huskily.

Jag mumbled something about finding his own wife before heading inside, but Rafe only had eyes for Alexa.

Kissing her again, he felt her move against him and groaned softly against her lips. 'You know accepting your marriage proposal was the best bargain I ever made, don't you?'

'You didn't accept my proposal,' Alexa scoffed. 'My father forced you to marry me.'

'Did he?' Rafe gave her an enigmatic look he knew would drive her crazy.

'Yes.' She glared at him. 'He did, didn't he?'

Rafe's grin widened. 'Have you ever known me to do anything that I didn't want to do?'

'No.' Her green gaze narrowed menacingly. 'Are you saying you wanted to marry me back then?'

'Let's just say no other man was ever going to have you after the way you kissed me that night.'

'You mean the way you kissed me,' she huffed.

'Want to argue about it inside?' he asked suggestively.

Alexa glanced anxiously over at the twins. 'How long do you think we have before the boys need us again?'

Rafe grabbed her hand and tugged her towards the Summer Palace. 'Long enough for me to show you how much I love you.'

'Oh, good.' Alexa's grin made his heart catch. 'My favourite thing.'

* * * * *

If you didn't want
Their Royal Wedding Bargain
to end, you won't be able
to resist these other stories
by Michelle Conder!

Defying the Billionaire's Command
The Italian's Virgin Acquisition
Bound to Her Desert Captor
The Billionaire's Virgin Temptation

Available now!